ALIEN LADDER

PETER WAUGH

WESTBOW
PRESS
A DIVISION OF THOMAS NELSON

WestBow Press books may be ordered through booksellers or by contacting:

WestBow Press
A Division of Thomas Nelson
1663 Liberty Drive
Bloomington, IN 47403
www.westbowpress.com
1 (866) 928-1240

Because of the dynamic nature of the Internet, any web addresses or
links contained in this book may have changed since publication and
may no longer be valid. The views expressed in this work are solely those
of the author and do not necessarily reflect the views of the publisher,
and the publisher hereby disclaims any responsibility for them.

Any people depicted in stock imagery provided by Thinkstock are models,
and such images are being used for illustrative purposes only.
Certain stock imagery © Thinkstock.

ISBN: 978-1-4908-0981-6 (sc)
ISBN: 978-1-4908-0980-9 (hc)
ISBN: 978-1-4908-0982-3 (e)

Library of Congress Control Number: 2013917365

Printed in the United States of America.

WestBow Press rev. date: 11/04/2013

To Margaret
My wife, friend and constant companion.

To our grandchildren
The Magnificent Seven
Chris, Cody and Cameron.
Abby, Sean, Matan and Ammiel.

Maureen Crooks
&
The children of Newbattle Sunday School
Past, Present and Future

IN MEMORY

KRISTINE A. MESERVE

RICH MARTIN

The Messenger

The sphere decelerated rapidly as it swept into an elliptical orbit around the planet. Invisible beams probed the surface below, seeking the coded response, but none came. It crossed over the night-shrouded hemisphere. Suddenly, a burst of activity flared up within the core of the sphere's guidance system. An answering signal was coming from the darkened planetary surface below.

CHAPTER 1

T HE EVENING BREEZE SWEPT TORMENTED flurries of drifting snow across the white slopes of Jake's Law. The lowlands of Scotland have several isolated, cone-shaped hills that jut up and dominate the surrounding terrain. Since ancient times, such hills have been called "laws." Six hundred foot-high Jake's Law was such a hill.

Alex Watts's wheezing breath billowed behind him in the chill night air. His gloved hand that hauled the sled's tow rope was numb with cold. He stopped, threw down the rope, and pulled an inhaler out of his anorak pocket. He shook it vigorously a couple of times, exhaled, closed his lips around the vent, and inhaled two quick puffs. Almost immediately he felt the tightness in his chest release. He took in a deep breath, quickly stuffing the inhaler back into his pocket. On the hillside below him, the dark silhouette of another figure stood out against the white slope. It was his best friend, Jim Hood, also dragging a sled as he slogged his way up the track that wound its way toward the summit of the law. Alex lifted his gaze upward. In all of his fourteen years, he had never seen so many stars, their visibility enhanced by the darkened streetlights of the village in the valley below. It was the one and only benefit of the strike.

It was the winter of 1984, a few days before Christmas, and the small, Scottish mining community of Newbattle, like the rest of the country, was experiencing the fourth month of the national coalminers' strike. Now the electricity workers had come out on a twelve-hour token work stoppage and power outage as a gesture of support.

Alex looked up at the Milky Way as he had never seen it before. Millions of stars, undimmed by the artificial lights of civilization, now pierced the velvety darkness of space. It reminded him of his first experience in a school play, standing on stage, dry-mouthed, heart thumping as the rising curtain revealed a growing expanse of strangers' eyes focusing on him from the darkened auditorium. Were strangers' eyes watching tonight from the vast auditorium of space?

Jim scrambled up alongside Alex, threw down his towrope, and slumped down heavily on his sled. "I'm knackered." He wiped a drop of moisture off the end of his nose with the back of his leather glove.

Alex sighed. "It was your idea." He looked up toward the summit of Jake's Law. "When we get to the top it will be downhill all the way home."

Jim groaned. "Let's just go from here."

Alex's response was cut short as a brilliant dot of light streaked across the heavens. "Meteor!" he shouted out, pointing upward.

Jim pivoted around just in time to see the object before it disappeared. "That wasn't a meteor; it was a shooting star."

"Rubbish! It was too big for that."

"Okay! Okay! Don't get your knickers in a twist," Jim scoffed. "I still think it was a shooting star."

"This one was different, Jim. It lasted a long time. Shooting stars are usually gone in a flash."

Jim rose up wearily, dusting the snow off his jeans. "Okay, Captain Kirk, if we are going to the top, let's do it. If the power comes back on, Mum promised to make fish and chips for dinner."

They continued their slogging climb. The snow became deeper and occasionally Alex's feet would break through the surface crust. They were breathing heavily when they crested the rise onto the summit, grateful to sit their weary bodies down on their sleds. The top of the law was roughly circular, just over one hundred and fifty-feet in diameter and almost flat. Standing out starkly against the snow-covered ground was a circle of ancient standing stones, known to the locals as "The Twelve Apostles." At the center of the circle stood the ruined walls of a small, medieval chapel.

Just then, necklaces of streetlights appeared in the valley below. Both boys let out a cheer. "Fish and chips, here I come," Jim shouted, slapping Alex on the back. "What are you having tonight? More rabbit food I suppose?"

Alex shoved him back. "Buzz off. Not everybody wants to stuff their face with deep-fried pizza."

The condensed breath of Alex's words still hung in the air when a small, hastily-shaped snowball struck him full in the chest. An impromptu snowball fight began, ending abruptly when Alex had to utilize his inhaler.

They sat silently together for a few minutes as the medication took effect.

Jim turned to look at him. "Are you okay?"

Alex held up his hand. "I'm fine! I'm fine! It's the cold air, that's all."

The two friends were different in many ways, especially

physically. It was, in fact, this difference that had been the cornerstone of their friendship. Years back, in primary school, their teacher, Miss MacDonald, had pulled them out before the rest of the class during a history lesson. She wished to demonstrate examples of some of the ancient tribal groups that had merged over the centuries to become the Scottish race. Alex, slim, tall, and fair, was a typical Celt. Jim, stocky, medium height, and dark-haired, was a Pict. Though her racial classification types may have been flawed, their classmates gleefully jumped on the concept and from then on referred to Alex and Jim as the "Flintstones." It was on this anvil of mutual humiliation that their friendship was forged. The friendship had long since outlasted the nickname.

They studied the scene below for some minutes. Almost every village house had a tiny multi-colored Christmas tree framed in one window. "I can't believe it's almost Christmas," said Jim. "Have you gotten a tree yet?"

"Not yet. My dad's been busy with the strike. He said he would pick one up tonight."

"It doesn't look like my dad is going to get back before Christmas," Jim sighed.

"Is he still in Saudi Arabia?"

"Yeah, some place called Jubail. It's on the Persian Gulf. He is installing some equipment. They are way behind schedule. He called Mum last night. He may get a flight home through Switzerland, but he says it's a long shot."

"He always brings you some neat stuff when he comes back from these jobs."

Jim shrugged. "I suppose." He glanced at Alex. "What are you getting for Christmas?"

"I don't know."

"I sent my list up the chimney last week."

Alex laughed. "You still do that?"

"It works, especially if I leave a copy around for Mum and Dad to find, just in case it doesn't make it out the chimney pot to old Santa." He grinned. "It works every time."

"My brother, Tom, and I used to do it." Alex's face clouded over. "Mum and Dad haven't been into Christmas much since he died."

"Your dad must be stressed out with all the strike stuff."

"Somebody threw a brick through our front window last night." Alex said, "Dad thinks it was some picketers from outside the area."

"But he's a union rep. He's on their side."

"He wants to come to an agreement and get the strike over with. Some of the local miners are getting fed up and want to get back to work."

Jim shook his head. "Mum says a lot of them have been turning up at the church food pantry all week. Things are getting a bit tight."

Alex looked toward the dark outline of Newbattle Parish Church on the outskirts of the village. A cross formed out of white light bulbs had been put atop the spire for the Christmas season. In the far distance he could see the floodlit, eighty foot-high pithead frame of Newbattle Colliery, the normally flickering spokes of the giant winding wheels stilled by the strike. Flakes of snow started to drift down around them. Down in the valley, the white diagonal bands of the storm had blanketed the lights of the village. Soon, only the tiny illuminated cross atop the church steeple was still visible. Jim jumped to his feet. "Let's get going before we get snowed in. I'm starving." He suddenly leaned his head to one side. "What's that?"

"What?" asked Alex.

"Can't you hear it?"

Then Alex heard it– a low, pulsing sound. He rose slowly to his feet. The sound grew louder by the second. It seemed to be coming from somewhere inside the stone circle. Jim was already cautiously edging toward the perimeter of the circle of stones.

Alex grabbed Jim's shoulder. "What are you doing?"

Jim shrugged his shoulder free from Alex's grip. "Don't be such a wimp. I just want to see what it is."

"It could be a German bomb left over from the war. They found one in London just a month ago."

Jim rolled his eyes. "Give me a break. The Jerries never bombed Newbattle." He turned and quickly moved up close to the nearest of the giant granite stones. Alex reluctantly joined him. Jim took a peek around the stone. "I think it's coming from the chapel." He moved out from behind the stone and cautiously stepped inside the open circle. Alex took a deep breath and followed. The pulsing sound was speeding up. Jim stopped in his tracks. "There's some kind of light in there."

Alex swallowed hard. The hairs on the back of his neck began to rise. There was a faint, greenish glow spilling out from the door and windows of the chapel, casting jagged shadows of the ruined walls across the snow-covered ground. The light was getting brighter. The pulsing sound continued to speed up. Alex grabbed Jim's arm. "We need to get out of here." Just then, the pulsating sound stopped. A narrow column of pale blue light streaked vertically upward from the heart of the ruin. Jim let out a yell of fear, jumped back, and collided with Alex, sending them both sprawling; Alex's eyes followed the shimmering column of light into the heavens. Then he saw it– a shining sphere, spiraling downward, as if attached by an invisible cord to the column of light. It was coming down right on top of them. Alex scrambled to get clear as a whirlwind tore at his clothes. Powdered snow swept up from the ground into his face and a violent blast of air flung him back to the ground.

The only sounds Alex could hear were the beating of his heart and the gentle moaning of the wind across the summit. He let out the breath he had been holding. He wiped off the thin layer of snow that covered his face and blinked away the moisture from his eyelashes. The column of light had vanished. The snow had stopped falling and stars reappeared. He slowly raised himself up on one elbow. Sitting still on the ground, close to the chapel, was the sphere, like a giant Christmas tree ornament, its mirror-like surface reflecting the snow and the stars. Jim crept alongside Alex, glistening from head to toe with a dusting of powdered snow. They both rose slowly to their feet.

The sphere was at least twelve feet in diameter. No markings of any kind blemished the mirror-like surface, which reflected their own distorted images back to them.

Jim's hands trembled as he wiped the snow off his face. "I'm getting out of here."

He took off in a stumbling run toward the summit rim. Alex, his heart beating like a hammer, was right behind him. There was a crackling sound. A bright blue light lit up the granite standing stones. Alex looked back over his shoulder. The column of light had once more thrust its way up into the heavens. The sphere had begun to roll along the ground. They scrambled the last few yards to the shelter of the nearest standing stone. Frightened, exhausted, and winded, the two terrified boys huddled together beside the rough granite block. The sphere was now rolling faster and faster around the chapel in ever increasing circles. It broke clear from the ground and spiraled up the blue column of light, carving a cylindrical path through the falling snow. Then it was gone. The light column was extinguished. Flakes of snow began to gently drift down around them.

They stood up and warily stepped out from behind the standing stone. Alex struggled to make sense of what he had seen. Had it all been a dream? Yet the circular track of the sphere's landing and takeoff was clearly imprinted in the snow. "Look!" Jim's voice was hoarse. A luminous cloud of gas, about the size of a large beach ball, was floating up above the ruined chapel. It rose higher and higher as a flickering blue light rippled across its luminous surface. Alex fumbled for his inhaler. It slipped out of his trembling fingers and fell to the ground. He dropped on one knee to pick it up. A flash of light streaked over his head. Jim let out a loud gasp. Alex turned around to see a thin beam of blue light connecting the ball of gas to Jim's chest. Jim seemed paralyzed. Then the beam was gone and Jim fell to his knees. Alex slowly stood up. He glanced at the cloud of gas out of the corner of his eye. Light was now rippling through it. It was changing shape, growing longer in a vertical direction.

He turned back to Jim. "Are you okay?"

Jim, still on his knees was rubbing his chest. "I couldn't move. I was stiff as a board." His eyes widened; Alex turned. The cloud was still changing shape.

"Let's get out of..." Alex's words died in his throat as a pencil thin beam of light streaked straight from the gas cloud and hit his chest. He felt no pain, just a dull numbness gripping his whole body. Then suddenly, the transfixing beam was gone. His body went loose. He staggered, but didn't fall. The gas cloud was rising higher and higher. Another thin beam streaked out from the cloud, passed right by the boys, and vanished over the rim of the hill. Suddenly, the air about them was laced with multiple beams of light. Both boys threw themselves flat on the hard-packed snow. Like some bizarre laser show, the cloud fired flickering beam after beam at an ever-increasing rate, all streaking down into the valley. Then, as suddenly as they had started, the beams stopped. Lights rippled across the surface of the gas cloud with increased intensity. It started to sink back down toward the chapel and disappeared out of sight behind the ruined walls. There was a sudden burst of light that spilled out the widows and the doorway, casting distorted shadows across the ground, then darkness. It was some moments until Alex's vision adjusted. He rubbed his eyes. A shadowy figure had stepped out of the chapel doorway and was walking slowly toward them.

CHAPTER 2

THEIR DESIRE WAS TO TURN and run, but their feet stayed rooted to the ground, their eyes fixed, as if in a trance, on the figure walking toward them.

"Hullo lads." The accent was Scottish; the dialect was local. The stranger had stopped a few yards from them. It was a man, average in height. Even in the poor light they could see the face was plain, without distinctive features. He was wearing a simple two-piece suit. "My name is Sus. Do not be afraid. I mean you no harm."

Alex released the breath he had been holding, "Pleased to meet you, Mr.Sus. I'm Alex Watts...and this is my friend, Jim Hood."

"Pleased to meet you, Alex Watts and Jim Hood. What is the name of this place?"

"Newbattle," said Jim.

"Newbattle?" Sus raised his eyebrows. "Where is London?"

Jim shook his head. "London is in England. This is Scotland."

"Scotland?" The stranger strolled over closer to the rim edge of the summit and looked down at the village below.

Jim grabbed hold of Alex's arm and whispered in his ear.

"This guy could be from MI5. It must be something to do with the strike."

"MI5! What about the blue light and the sphere and all that stuff?"

Jim shrugged. "It's some new technology. My uncle says the government has a bunch of secret stuff they don't tell us about. What else could it be?"

"He could be from outer space."

"Outer space?" Jim scoffed. "You heard his accent. More like outer Glasgow. Anyway, if you think he's an alien, why are you still standing here?" Alex did feel unexpectedly calm. Jim was always pulling his leg about being a "worry wart." His hands had been trembling just minutes ago. Now they were steady. He walked over to join the stranger who was still staring at the village below. Jim, after some hesitation, followed after him.

Sus turned. "I need to go to London. I have important information to give to your government."

"The Scottish Parliament is in Edinburgh," said Alex.

"How do I get there?"

"There is a bus from the village every hour."

Would you take me to the village? Time is short. Do you have a vehicle here?"

Alex pointed to the sleds, "We have those."

Sus frowned. "What is the method of propulsion?"

Jim sniggered. "Propulsion? It's a sled, mister. What do you..."

"It can only go downhill," Alex interrupted.

A fleeting smile flickered across Sus's face. "Ah! I understand. Whose sled do I travel on?"

Jim spoke up. "Alex can take you. He has more room. I'll lead the way."

Alex stepped over to his sled and picked up the tow rope. "Just sit on the back Mr. Sus. I will sit on the front and steer with my feet. You need to hold on to me. It might get bumpy."

Sus nodded and sat on the rear of the sled. Alex wound the towrope around his gloved hand and sat on the front. Sus's legs were on either side of Alex, his hands rested lightly on Alex's shoulders.

"Are you ready?" called out Jim, who was already kneeling on the rear of his sled at the top of the track, ready to push off.

"Let's go." Alex tucked the rope under him and took a firm hold of the bar with both hands. Jim pushed the sled for a few steps and then threw himself on top and vanished over the lip of the slope. Alex took a deep breath and pushed off by digging his heel into the snow. The sled slid over the lip down onto the track and accelerated into the darkness. The metal runners hissed through the snow and each time he dug in his heels to steer, a fine spray of ice would sting his face. He had to keep blinking to clear his eyes. Ahead, he could just make out the dark speeding shape of Jim, stretched out belly-down on his sled, throwing up a fantail of powdered snow as he negotiated the curves in the trail. Jim made a sweeping turn to the left. Alex dug in his left heel. The sled tipped over on one runner for a second, drawing dangerously close to the drop off. Alex threw his weight to the other side and the sled dropped back on even keel. The streetlights were close. They were rapidly approaching the rear of the village pub, "The Justinlees Inn." The trail had flattened out and their speed had begun to taper off. They swept past the inn and Alex's teeth jarred together as the sled crossed the sidewalk and dropped onto the ice-packed roadway. Alex shouted, "Are you okay, Mister Sus?"

"Yes," was the curt reply. Now they were near the center

of the village. Fortunately, there was no traffic, but some cars were parked along the sides of the road and he had to steer down the middle. His legs were aching with the strain and the smooth packed down ice made the overloaded sled difficult to control. As they came to another bend in the road, Alex could see a group of people up ahead milling about under a street light. Jim was now only a few feet in front. A man, arms flailing wildly, had broken away from the group and staggered across the street. Light reflected off something shiny in his hand. A jeering bunch of youths ran after him, oblivious to the approaching sleds. Jim yelled out a warning at the top of his lungs. His sled started to skid to one side. Alex dug both heels in. His sled began to fishtail. He tried to correct it, but it was too late. Sideways on, they ploughed into the milling throng. Bodies, beer cans, and curses filled the night. The sled hit the curb side on, launching its riders into the air. Alex's head struck hard and stars exploded before his eyes.

CHAPTER 3

ALEX OPENED HIS EYES. THE back of his head throbbed painfully. He gingerly moved his arms and legs. Everything seemed to be working.

Then he heard the growing sounds of angry voices rising in the frosty air. There was the crunch of feet on the frozen snow. Rough hands grabbed the front of his anorak and dragged him to his feet. Beer tainted breath wafted into his nostrils.

"Well if isnae Alex Watts..." Alex recognized the voice before he made out the chiseled features of Nick Stoddart, five years older than Alex, and the village tough guy. A semi-circle of shadowy figures appeared behind him.

"You almost killed us you little git," Stoddart continued, twisting his grip on the anorak making the collar cut into Alex's throat. "How's your yellow-belly dad doing?" Alex struggled to break free. A violent shove sent him rolling over the frozen ground colliding into somebody's feet. He looked up. It was Sus.

"These are my friends," Sus spoke quietly.

"Well what have we here lads? The Lone Ranger?" There was a ripple of jeering laughter from Stoddart's cohorts.

He stepped closer to Sus. "And who would you be, you wee squirt?"

"My name is Sus and I have..."

Stoddart suddenly threw a punch. Sus stepped back. Stoddart's fist cut harmlessly through the air. He lost his balance, tripped and fell to the ground. Some of his gang sniggered out loud. Stoddart let loose a stream of obscenities as he scrambled to his feet. "Okay you, now you're asking for it." He grabbed hold of the front of Sus's coat with his left hand and raised his balled right fist above his head. Sus grabbed both lapels of Stoddart's jacket and pulled the youth's face hard down on to his skull. There was a sickening dull crunch. Stoddert let out a scream of pain and staggered back clutching his nose.

Jim let out a gasp, "A head-butt!" He grabbed Alex's arm. "He didn't learn that on Mars." Stoddart's gang members stood in shocked silence, watching their leader stumbling around, moaning pitifully with blood dripping through his fingers, forming dark stains on the snow-covered ground.

Sus stood staring at Stoddart with a confused look on his face. He turned to Alex, "Why did I do that?"

Alex grabbed his arm. "We need to get out of here fast."

It was too late. Stoddart's companions had overcome their initial shock and were beginning to form a threatening circle around Sus, Alex, and Jim. Just then, someone shouted out, "It's the police! Run for it!" The sounds of running feet were drowned out by the strident noise of a police siren and a pulsating blue light flickering across the scene.

Two uniformed officers jumped out. A flashlight beam picked out Alex's face. "What's going on here?" He recognized the voice of Police Constable Bill Brown. His father, Sergeant Brown, was the senior officer at the village station. Unlike his father, P.C. Bill Brown had a good rapport with the younger residents of Newbattle. The other policeman approached, leading a disheveled older man behind him. P.C. Brown turned his flashlight on the newcomer, "Och! It's you Mr. Adams."

The old man leaned closer and fixed his bleary eyes on the policeman. "Brown. Billy Brown is it?" He slurred the words. He clumsily dusted the snow off his crumpled overcoat, spilling liquid from the bottle he had in his hand.

The other policeman suddenly noticed Sus. "Who's this guy?"

Jim stepped forward, "His name is Sus. We found him on Jake's Law. He came down out of the sky in some kind of satellite. He wants to go to Edinburgh to talk to the government. We ran into Stoddart and his mob. They were messing around with old Adams. This guy head-butted Stoddart. It was brilliant. I think he's from MI5 or something, but Alex thinks he's from outer space."

Alex protested, "He has come to warn us about something."

P.C. Brown held up his hand. "Okay lads, joke's over. Any more smart comments and you'll get my boot on your rear ends." He shone his flashlight on Sus's face. "Who are you sir?"

"My name is Sus."

"You don't look like the head-butting type, Mr. Sus. What were you doing on top of Jake's Law on a night like this?"

"I am from the planet Ven. I have come to warn your world that it is in danger. It is soon to be attacked by an invading fleet from the far side of the galaxy. I need to speak to your leaders."

P.C. Brown sighed. "Tell me, Mr. Sus, did you pay a visit to the Justinlees Inn this evening?"

The car radio burst into crackling life. The other

policeman ran back to the Rover and grabbed the mike from the dashboard. "Baker Charlie." The reply was another burst of staccato sounds. "Roger, Baker Charlie out," he whirled around. "Come on, Bob, sarge wants us back at the station right away."

P.C. Brown took Sus by the arm. "We better take Mr. Adams and this chap back with us." They helped the old man into the back seat of the Rover, then bundled Sus in after him.

Adams put his arm around Sus. "How are you doing pal? Merry Christmas to ye. How about a wee drap of whisky, eh?" Some liquid slopped out of the bottle onto Sus.

The two policemen jumped into the front seats. The Rover's engine burst into life. P.C. Brown rolled down the window. "Why don't you two kids follow us down to the station?" He smiled. "You can explain to my dad how you found ET here." Spinning tires threw up a spray of powdered ice as the Rover did a sharp u-turn and roared off up the street.

Alex and Jim watched the receding red rear lights of the Rover. Raised voices floated through the night air. Stoddart and his gang were still in the area. The two teenagers launched their sleds down the gently sloping street toward the police station.

A few minutes later, they entered the brightly lit front office of the station. Sergeant Brown was behind the counter writing up a report. He seemed unaware of the entrance of the boys. Voices echoed down through the corridor that led to the detention cells. Alex recognized the voice of Bill Brown. The other voice was that of Mr. Adams, but it seemed different. The phone on the counter buzzed. The sergeant lifted the receiver. "Police Station - Sergeant Brown..." There was a babble of words from the other end of the line. He jumped to his feet. "I'll get somebody down there right away." He slammed the phone back on the receiver. "Bill! Frank! Get in here."

There was a clatter of boots in the corridor and the two policemen rushed into the reception area. "What's up, Dad?" said Bill breathlessly.

"There's trouble down at the coal mine. A bunch of picketers are trying to break through the main gates. You better get down there right away." He pointed down the corridor. "What about those two you brought in?"

Bill Brown took off his peaked cap and ran his fingers through his curly red hair. "It's the queerest thing. Old Adams is back there stone cold sober. When we picked him up, he was sloshed. Now he's asking what happened. I called Mrs. Adams and she's coming to take him home."

"What about the other fellow?"

His son shook his head. "He doesn't have any identification. No wallet. No money. Nothing, except a wee box with some silver marbles in it." He paused for a moment. "He seems to be a bit confused." P.C. Brown turned toward Alex and Jim. "Luke Skywalker and Hans Solo here say he landed on top of Jake's Law in a UFO. He says he's from another planet and has come to save us. Apparently he gave Nick Stoddart a 'Glasgow kiss.' I have a hunch he's involved in the strike in some way. He's probably had a few drinks, but he could be concussed. We should get him looked at by Dr. Bruce."

Sergeant Brown's face flushed. "We've no time for all this rubbish. Get down to the pit before they start a riot. I'll phone to Edinburgh and get some help sent out from headquarters."

Bill Brown turned to Alex and Jim. "Look you two, do me a favor and take ET here along to Dr. Bruce's surgery and ask him to check him out. Ask the doc to hold onto him and I will pick him up later." He shouted the last few words over his shoulder as he and Frank ran out the front door.

Just then, the desk phone rang. Sergeant Brown grabbed it. "Newbattle Police Station." He listened for a few moments, nervously tapping his pencil on the counter top. "Okay then, Mrs. Adams, see you soon."

He replaced the phone and just as he did, it rang again. He groaned and snatched it back up. "Hold on a sec." He placed his hand over the mouthpiece and turned to the teenagers. "You two go back and tell Mr. Adams that his wife will be here in ten minutes." He glanced up at the wall clock. "Then go home," he paused, "and while you're at it, you can drop your wee friend at Dr. Bruce's surgery like Bill suggested."

Alex and Jim walked slowly down the corridor leading to the cells. Mr. Adams was sitting on a seat outside the first cell, rubbing his temples with both hands. He looked up and gave them a bemused smile. Alex had never been one to make a fool of Mr. Adams since his father told him about the car accident that had taken the life of Mr. and Mrs. Adams's only son. Mr. Adams had been driving and had blamed himself for the tragedy.

"How are you feeling, Mr. Adams?" asked Alex.

The old man shook his head. "I feel fine lad, but I don't know how I got here." He looked at Alex with eyes that were clear and steady. "I'm heading home in a bit."

Alex nodded. " Yes, Sergeant Brown says to tell you that Mrs. Adams is coming to pick you up in ten minutes." They headed for the next cell. The door was wide open. Alex took a cautious look inside. Sus was sitting on the bunk holding his head in his hands. "P.C. Brown wants us to take you to the doctor. He thinks you may have injured your head." Taking an arm cach the two boys gently raised Sus up from the bunk.

Sus did not speak. It was the first time they had seen him in good light. His suit was a grey, lightweight material and his shoes were also grey. He had a pleasant, but very ordinary face and rather mousey brown hair. No distinctive features except for his eyes. They were a light, almost luminous blue, but they seemed focused on something far, far away.

A few minutes later, they were walking down the street supporting Sus, one on each side and towing their sleds with their free hand. As they drew near Dr. Bruce's surgery, they could see his Land Rover parked outside the front door. They stopped at the front gate. "What do we tell Dr. Bruce?" said Jim.

"What do you mean?"

"Like should we be telling him how we saw Sus land up on the law in a weird sphere and that he says he's from another planet?" Jim responded with some irritation.

Alex shook his head. "I don't think so Jim. Nobody has believed us so far. Sus has to be the one to convince them who he is, but he can't in the condition he's in now."

Jim nodded. "I suppose you're right. That's what we get for being teenagers. No respect. We're lucky if they notice we exist half the time."

Just then, the front door flew open and the rotund figure of Dr. Bruce ran down the path toward the Land Rover, still in the process of hauling on his overcoat. "Are you lads looking for me?" His tone was irritable.

"Yes, Dr. Bruce." Alex dropped his sled rope. "We found this man on the top of Jake's Law. He had a bit of an accident. P.C. Brown wants you to have a look at him. He might have hit his head."

The doctor threw his medical bag into the back seat and moved toward Sus. "Bring him under the street light and let's have a look. Be quick about it. I've only got a minute. The village is having an attack of mass hysteria."

"What's happening?" asked Alex. He had never seen the doctor so flustered.

"Folk are having bad turns all over the place. I have seen seven already. They all thought they were having heart attacks. They were all perfectly healthy when I checked them out. Some said they had got struck by lightning. It's the strike that's to blame. Everyone is getting stressed out and neurotic."

Alex and Jim exchanged looks. The doctor pulled a thin flashlight out of his jacket pocket and took a close look at Sus's face. "He's not from around here. He might be one of the flying pickets from out of town." He leaned forward. "His pupils are dilated." He sniffed, sighed loudly, swung round, and headed back to the Land Rover. He jumped in and slammed the door.

Alex followed after him. "What's wrong with him, Dr. Bruce?"

The doctor slid back the window. "There is no sign of a head injury. I can smell alcohol and he is showing some symptoms of intoxication. He was probably at the Justinlees Inn like some of my patients that thought they had been struck by lightning. They must be selling bad beer. I have an emergency situation and I need to leave. If you want to be good Samaritans, take him round to the Salvation Army so he can get out of the cold and sleep it off." He turned on the ignition and the Land Rover sped off into the darkness.

Alex turned just in time to see Sus slide down the lamppost onto the ice-covered pavement. They each took an arm and pulled him back upright. Sus's eyes were open but unseeing, as if in a trance. Jim sniffed. "There is a smell of whisky on him. Maybe old Adams gave him a slug out of his bottle in the police car."

Alex shivered. The temperature was dropping as the evening wore on. "Nobody's listening to us, Jim. What do we do?"

Jim shrugged, "I already told you. They think kids our age are retarded." He glanced down the street. The small illuminated cross floated above the pointed pyramid steeple atop the square 16th century tower of Newbattle Church. "Why don't we take him to the church?"

"How would that help?" asked Alex.

"The Salvation Army place is too far away. I need to be getting home. My mum will be having a fit. I think Mr. Dickson would help. He's a minister after all."

"Why would he believe, Jim? Nobody else does."

"Well, he tells us all the Bible stuff and he expects us to believe him."

Alex considered Jim's suggestion for a few moments. It might work. He liked Reverend Dickson. His parents had rarely attended church and in 1981, when his older brother Tom died, they had stopped altogether. Jim's mother did some volunteer secretarial work for Reverend Stuart Dickson, and occasionally Alex would go to the Sunday service with Jim and his parents. In the three years he had been minister of Newbattle Parish Church, forty-five year old Dickson had achieved more success with the young people of the village than with the grownups. He had started various youth activities, including a model aircraft club, which Alex and Jim attended. He had recently firmed up his appeal to the younger members of the congregation by playing the Tina Turner record, "What's love got to do with it?" to enhance one of his sermons. It had not, however, enhanced his standing with many of the more senior members of the congregation. If any adult was going to give them a fair hearing, it would be Reverend Dickson.

CHAPTER 4

AFTER STOWING THEIR SLEDS BEHIND the doctor's garden wall, they set off along the road toward the church. Sus, though still uncommunicative, was able to walk with their support. Next door to the church was the eighteenth century manse. Every window was lit up. Lights were also on in the church. The stained glass cast a dappled mosaic of colors across the snow-covered sidewalk and street. "Something must be going on," said Alex.

"I just remembered," said Jim. "There's a communion service tonight."

"I thought that was on Christmas Eve?" said Alex.

"This is a special service to pray for the end of the strike," said Jim. A low wall ran across the front of the manse and the church. The original wrought iron fence and gates had been removed in 1939 to help the war effort. They had never been replaced. They were both breathing heavily with their efforts to support Sus. "Let's sit him on the wall for a minute," gasped Jim. "I'm clapped out." Alex nodded agreement. They dusted the thin layer of snow off the top of the wall and wearily sat down with Sus supported between them. They took a few moments to get their breath back. On the opposite side of the road was the twelve foot-high Monkland Wall, and behind it the grounds of Newbattle Abbey. The monks had built the wall in the tenth century all the way around their property.

"I heard that Fiona Dickson has been really sick," said Alex.

Jim nodded. "She's been off school for weeks."

Alex looked over his shoulder toward the manse and shivered. "Let's get on with it. I'm freezing."

Jim groaned, "We don't have to drag him over there. You go and I'll stay here and keep an eye on him." Alex, too tired to argue, got up and walked toward the front door of the manse. His feet crunched through the thin covering of the recent snow into the granite gravel chips. He pulled the old style bell knob. A distant jangling came from the inner depths of the manse. A tall figure appeared behind the frosted glass upper panels of the door. It opened to reveal Reverend Dickson. The angular face, the thick, lank, black hair streaked with grey, all atop the lanky frame, always reminded Alex of the movie star, James Stewart.

"Well, hello there, Alex. What can we do for you?" The minister's usual friendly smile was present but there was weariness about his eyes.

"I have something to tell you, Mr. Dickson. Something we need help with..." Just then, the phone on the hallstand behind Mr. Dickson burred into life. The minister turned quickly to look at the instrument. The bell continued its strident call but he made no move toward it. A small, attractive, dark haired woman appeared in the hall. It was Rose Dickson, her flour covered hands playing with the apron tied around her waist. She didn't seem to notice Alex.

"You better answer it, Stuart," she said softly.

Her husband stepped over to the phone and picked it up. He cleared his throat.

"Hello, Stuart Dickson here...Oh, yes, Dr. Bruce...What's the news?" He listened in silence, his free hand rubbing his forehead. "There is no doubt then?" His voice was flat. "No! No! Dr. Bruce. We need to know. You will call in later then? Goodnight." He slowly replaced the phone. A moment passed before he looked at his wife. Then he remembered Alex, "Oh! Sorry old chap." He took a deep breath. "Look, if your problem isn't too critical, I would be grateful if you could check back with me later. We have a bit of a family emergency going on."

Alex nodded, "Sorry. I'll come back later on."

"That's good of you, Alex. See you later then." The door closed behind Alex as he walked back to the gate. He turned to look at the manse. He could see the distorted shapes of the minister and his wife behind the frosted glass. They were hugging each other. He joined Jim and Sus.

"How did it go?" asked Jim.

"I think Fiona must be doing badly. Dr. Bruce called when I was over there. Mr. Dickson asked me to come back later."

Jim sighed. "It's like a game of 'Pass then Parcel.' Every time the music stops, we still have him. Now what do we do?"

Alex shook his head, "I think Mr. Dickson will listen to us when he has time, but we need to get Sus out of the cold."

Jim suddenly banged his hands together. "I've got it! The stable's loft."

A few minutes later they had carried Sus around to the rear of the church. The stables formed part of a separate building that had, in bygone years, sheltered the minister's horse and buggy. One half, which had housed the buggy, now was a garage for Mr. Dickson's red Mini. The other half, which had been the horse stalls, had been converted into a small meeting room for the children's Sunday school. During World War II, the stable's loft served as a billet for the soldiers manning the antiaircraft gun emplacement on top of Jake's Law. They had constructed a wooden staircase on the outside of the building to give easier access.

Alex and Jim awkwardly carried Sus up the steep steps. The door was unlocked, but the rusty hinges and snow on the landing required some effort from Alex and Jim before they were able to push it open. They hustled Sus through the narrow door into the dark, dusty interior of the loft. Jim heeled the door closed behind them. He pulled a small pen flashlight out of his pocket and flicked it on.

The attic had provided cramped accommodation for the soldiers who had been billeted there all those years ago. The wooden bunks were still in place along the center where headroom was the greatest. They were piled high with old hymnbooks, picture frames, and cardboard boxes of all shapes and sizes. Alex held on to Sus while Jim cleared one of the bunks. The dust floated freely in the light beam. Alex sneezed several times. He patted his pockets to locate his inhaler. The old mattress was dusty and torn, but surprisingly dry. They eased Sus down onto the bunk. His eyes were closed, but his breathing was steady.

"Well, what do we do now?" asked Jim.

"Just let him rest for a bit, I suppose," said Alex.

"I still think we need to let the grownups handle this." Jim's hand that held the penlight was shaking slightly.

"I'm scared as well, Jim."

Jim snapped back, "Who says I'm scared? You're the nervous one. I don't spend all my time reading science fiction magazines and watching Dr. Who."

"You don't read anything, Jim."

"I can't help that. The school counselor says I've got DDT."

"You mean ADD?"

Jim shrugged. "Whatever! Dad says it's a lot of rubbish. Just an excuse for bad teachers."

There was an awkward silence. Jim glanced at the dark shape on the bunk. "If he is really from some other planet, he may have come to take over Earth. Just like that old 'War of the Worlds' movie."

"If that's the case, he's gotten off to a bad start."

Jim tried to hold back a snigger but failed. "He's not exactly Darth Vader." They both laughed and the tension lifted.

Alex grew more serious. "I don't think he means us harm, Jim. He came here for some important reason."

Then they heard a creaking sound from outside.

"Someone's coming up the stairs," Jim whispered. He switched off the penlight.

Alex's mouth had gone very dry. The creaking continued, getting closer all the time. Then it stopped. Alex could feel his heart pounding. The door creaked open very slowly. A small, hooded figure, dressed in white, stood there, framed in the doorway.

"What are you lot up to?" The clear, matter of fact voice deflated the tension like a pin pricking a balloon.

Jim flicked on the penlight. "It's Fiona Dickson..."

Fiona's pale face framed in the hood of her white anorak looked thin and pinched, contrasting with the dark brown, intelligent eyes. A tuft of dark hair hung down across her forehead. Below the anorak was the lace-trimmed hem of a nightgown. She wore white wellington boots. She stepped inside. "Who is that?" She pointed toward the dark shape on the bunk. The boys exchanged looks with each other. "I saw you from my bedroom window. I saw you bring him up here. Who is he?"

"Okay!" said Jim. "But you won't believe us."

"Try me. I'm not as stupid as you think."

"You better close the door," said Alex. Jim pulled the door shut. Alex launched into a description of the events that had led up to the present situation. When he finished, Jim turned the fading beam of the flashlight on the girl's face.

"I think he is working for the government. Out to break the strike. Alex thinks he's from Mars or something." Her eyes were wide open and her lower lip hung down. She looked at the boys in turn, and then walked across to the bunk. One of Sus's arms had slipped to the floor. She gingerly picked it up and laid it across his chest.

"He just looks like a man," she said.

"That's what I think," said Jim.

Just then a door slammed somewhere outside. Jim flicked off his flashlight and pushed the door open a crack to look out.

"Who is it, Jim?" Alex whispered.

"It's Fiona's mum and dad. They're walking across to the church."

Fiona moved quickly to the door. "I have to get back to my room." She turned toward Alex. "I saw the blue column of light on Jake's Law just for a few seconds. I told Mum and Dad. When they looked, the snow had started falling and they couldn't see anything. I think they thought I was having a fever or something." She turned to Jim. "If the government wanted to send somebody here secretly, why would they send him here in a silver sphere that spirals down a beacon of light that shoots up out of Jake's Law? It doesn't make sense." She moved toward the door. "Leave the wee man here. No one will come up. I will keep checking on him. After the evening service, we will get a chance to talk to Dad." She stepped out into the night, pulling the door closed behind her.

Jim turned to Alex. "Can you believe that? She's only thirteen. Who is she to boss us around? Just 'cause she lives in a posh manse."

"I think she's right though, Jim. He is still out for the count. We should get home. My folks will be worried if I don't get back soon. So will your mum. We can meet when the church service is over, like she said."

"Are you going to tell them about Sus?" asked Jim.

"I think we need to wait till he can explain what it's all about."

Jim nodded. "You're right. They'd think we had been sniffing glue. Ever since Mum got that booklet from the school on drug addiction, she's always watching me for symptoms. I sometimes feel like one of those laboratory rats."

"We could meet back here after dinner," said Alex.

Jim shrugged. "I have to go to the service with Mum, but I might be able to sneak out."

Alex looked at the figure on the bunk. "He will get really cold up here. We need to find something else to keep him warm."

A short search produced an old khaki army overcoat which was in a cupboard. It smelt a bit musty, but it was surprisingly dry considering how long it had been hanging there. Together, they got Sus buttoned up in to it. They carefully laid him back down on the mattress, opened the loft door, and slipped outside. There was nobody in sight, so they quickly descended the stairs and went to pick up their sleds.

Ten minutes later, Alex pulled his sled down McLean Place, heading for home. Jim had already branched off for his house, which was on the other side of the village. There was the sound of running feet. A group of men were heading down the street toward him. The sound of a police siren split the still night air. Flickering blue lights appeared at the far end of the street. The group of men suddenly scattered and dispersed down side alleys. One jumped over a garden wall just in front of Alex. The police car raced up the street, skidded on the ice, and swerved down a side road.

Alex shook his head and trudged on homeward. Such incidents had become commonplace as the miners' strike continued its bitter course. Alex was only too aware of the pressures building up in the village. His father was an official in the miners' union. Alex had experienced some harassment from a few classmates whose fathers disagreed with Mr. Watts's efforts to resolve the strike. He turned onto McLean Place. There was another police car in front of his house. Debris littered the roadway. He started to run. One of the lower floor windows was broken. A low brick wall bordered the small front garden and on it, marked out in yellow spray paint, was a crude sign. Even in the darkness, Alex could clearly read the words: "WATTS IS A DIRTY SCAB."

CHAPTER 5

ALEX SLOWED DOWN AS HE drew near the police car. It was empty but he could hear the radio relaying staccato bursts of communication between other cars and headquarters. He looked at the number plate. It was not a local police vehicle. He pushed open the small wooden gate. It scraped along the ground on one hinge. He kicked away a beer can that was lying on the path. Liquid fanned out from it as it spun into the darkness. The front door's paint was chipped and scarred. Stones and broken bottles lay all around. He was reaching out for the door handle when the door suddenly swung open.

His father stood there, a look of relief on a face lined and marked by years working down the coal mine. "Where have you been? Your mother was getting worried." He ran calloused fingers through his thinning gray hair. He ushered Alex into the hall and closed the door quickly behind him.

"What happened, Dad?" asked Alex, hanging his anorak on the coat stand.

"Just a few nut cases from the picket line down at the pit. If their brains were gunpowder, they wouldn't have enough to blow their hats off." His father pushed open the kitchen door.

"Is that Alex?" His mother's anxious voice came from inside.

His father ushered him into the kitchen. "Yes, Jessie. He's fine."

Alex blinked in the light. Two policemen were sitting at the table, drinking tea and eating scones. He did not recognize either of them. His mother was in the process of topping up the teapot with boiling water. "We've been worried sick, especially with all the trouble going on. What were you thinking about?"

Alex shrugged. "Sorry, Mum. Jim and I were sledding on Jake's Law. Forgot about the time."

"Did you have your inhaler with you?"

"Yes, Mum. I always have it with me."

His mother took a mug out of the cupboard and brought it over to the table. "Sit yourself down. You must be chilled to the bone."

He sat down beside the policemen. As his mother poured out the tea, he noticed that underneath her apron she was wearing her good two-piece tweed suit. His father also sat down at the table. He was also wearing his best charcoal grey suit. It would have passed for new except for its style and the faint odor of mothballs. One of the policemen picked up the plate of scones and offered it to Alex. "Have one of these, lad, before they vanish. Their goodness has been the death of them as my old mother used to say."A brief smile lit up Mrs. Watts's drawn, but still attractive face. The policeman was rewarded with a topping up of his teacup. He looked toward the sideboard. Several tarnished trophy cups, and some shiny and polished were on display. Alongside were a few framed photographs of football teams. "I remember watching you play for the Arniston Rangers at the East of Scotland Junior

Cup Final, Mr. Watts. I was just the same age as your lad here." He smiled at Alex. "Those new shiny ones must be yours, Alex. Are you a right winger like your old dad?"

There was an awkward moment of silence. Alex busied himself spreading jam on his scone.

Mr. Watts nervously cleared his throat. "Those belong to our older son, Tom. He won them when he was in high school."

"What's he doing now?

Mr. Watts cast a quick glance at his wife. "Tom joined the Royal Marines when he left high school. We lost him in the Falklands."

The policeman's face reddened, "Sorry. I didn't know." He took a quick sip of tea.

Alex glanced at the framed picture of Tom in his Royal Marine uniform on the mantelpiece above the fireplace. When Tom had sailed with the British fleet for the Falkland Islands, his mother had a big candle burning on the mantelpiece next to Tom's picture. The candle had long since gone, but the soot mark on the ceiling remained.

He and Tom had been almost eight years apart in age. Tom's success in sports had been a great source of pride to his parents, particularly Mr. Watts. Alex, limited by asthma and not so gifted athletically, struggled in the shadow of his big brother. This had led to a less than close relationship between them, especially in Alex's early teen years. However, when Tom returned home after his marine basic training, things had been different. Tom's previously sarcastic comments were replaced with words of encouragement and support. Alex's envy and resentment drained away. Now Tom was gone.

Alex took a bite of jam filled scone. "What are you dressed

up for, Mum?" he asked, spraying out a few crumbs in the process.

"Don't speak with your mouth full. How often do I need to tell you?" She removed her apron. "I have to go upstairs. Your dad can explain what's going on. We are leaving for Edinburgh in a few minutes." She gave his father a meaningful look as she left the room. Mr. Watts stood up and patted his pockets. He pulled out a packet of cigarettes and offered them to the policemen. Both accepted and some seconds passed as they performed the lighting ritual.

"Sorry about bringing up about your son, Tom, and upsetting your wife, Mr. Watts."

Mr. Watts inhaled deeply, held it for a moment, then slowly exhaled. "Don't worry about that constable. Jessie didn't want Tom to go down the mine. Her brother was killed in a pit accident years ago. She was happy with him going into the Marines, but then…." He walked over to the kitchen window and slid it up a few inches, before turning to Alex. "As your mother said, we're off to Edinburgh. The officers are going to take us. It's a special union meeting."

Alex glanced at the policemen, "Why don't you go in our car?"

His father flicked his ash into the sink and turned on the tap to flush it away. "Well, after what happened tonight, we need some protection from the lunatic fringe. They think I am too soft and that I will be voting to end the strike tonight and sell the workers down the river."

"Why is Mum going with you?"

"We will be staying overnight in the town. She's nervous about all that's going on and I didn't want her left here on her own." He took another quick puff at his cigarette. "We know you wouldn't want to hang around a hotel, so we arranged for you to stay at the Hood's."

Alex stood at the Hood's front door, watching the rear lights of the police car carrying his parents recede into the night. In his hand he was still clutching the five pound note his father had slipped him.

Mrs. Hood and Jim stood beside him. Mrs. Hood took Alex's arm. "Come away into the house, and we'll have some dinner. I hope you like fish and chips, Alex?" They entered the warmth of the house to be met by the appetizing aroma that wafted through the kitchen door. A six-foot Christmas tree filled one corner of the living room, covered with shiny ornaments and flashing fairy lights. Colored paper chains spread out from the central ceiling light to the corners of the room. Christmas cards hung by small plastic pegs from a green string draped along the mantelpiece. The fireplace, stacked with kindling and coal, was unlit. A plain, two-barred electric fire glowed from the hearth. Mrs. Hood was saving the therapeutic effect of the real coal fire for Christmas Eve. The strike had drastically affected supplies.

Soon, they were sitting down at the table with plates of golden battered fish and chips. The warm food relaxed the tension that had clutched Alex's insides. For a moment, he had forgotten all about the stranger lying in the stable's loft. When they had consumed the last morsels, Mrs. Hood started to gather the empty plates. "Now, we will have a cup of tea and a nice bit of fruitcake." As she left the room, Mrs. Hood glanced at the clock on the mantelpiece. "Ah, time for the news. Jim, be a good lad and switch on the telly." Jim got up and leaned over to switch on the television. The screen flickered into life and the familiar face of the male newsreader appeared.

"...AND NOW FOR SOME LOCAL NEWS. THE MINERS' STRIKE REACHED NEW HEIGHTS OF VIOLENCE TODAY IN MANY PARTS OF THE COUNTRY. TEAMS OF FLYING PICKETS ATTEMPTED TO OCCUPY THE OFFICE FACILITIES IN SEVERAL LOCAL COALMINES. ONE OF THESE WAS NEWBATTLE COLLIERY WHERE THE CONFRONTATION BETWEEN THE PICKETS AND THE POLICE IS STILL IN PROGRESS. THE USE OF THE FLYING PICKETS HAS BECOME A CONTROVERSIAL SUBJECT WITHIN THE MINERS' UNION. MODERATES BELIEVE THE USE OF SUCH TACTICS LEADS TO VIOLENCE AND HAS A NEGATIVE EFFECT ON THE UNION'S IMAGE WITH THE PUBLIC."

Mrs. Hood bustled in from the kitchen with a plate of sliced fruitcake in one hand and a large teapot in the other. She stopped and pointed at the screen. "There's the man I don't trust." Everybody looked at the screen. A crowd of placard bearing pickets was grouped around a tall, sharp-featured man being interviewed by the TV reporter.

"I HAVE WITH ME MR. VICTOR STEEL, THE NATIONAL ORGANIZER OF THE FLYING PICKETS WHO IS JUST ABOUT TO LEAVE FOR EDINBURGH TO ATTEND A SPECIAL MEETING OF UNION LEADERS." He pointed the microphone to the union man. "WHY HAS THIS MEETING BEEN CALLED, MR. STEEL? WE HAVE HEARD THAT STRONG DIVISIONS ARE FORMING WITHIN THE UNION AND THAT A SETTLEMENT OF

THE STRIKE COULD BE WITH US ANY TIME NOW. IS THAT HOW YOU SEE IT?"

Steel gave a thin-lipped smile. His neatly trimmed black mustache twitched slightly before he answered.

"THIS IS NOT A FIGHT FOR MORE MONEY BUT FOR THE RIGHTS OF DECENT, HARD WORKING PEOPLE, TO BE GAINFULLY EMPLOYED."

A burst of applause broke out in the ranks of the pickets. Steel turned to acknowledge the support with a wave of his gloved hand. "THERE ARE SOME FENCE SITTERS IN THE STRIKE COMMITTEE WHO HAVE BEEN CONNED BY THE TORY CONTROLLED PRESS AND HAVE REQUESTED ANOTHER VOTE ..."

Mrs. Hood sighed loudly. "Try another channel Jim. We need a change from the strike." Jim clicked the channel control. An attractive lady newsreader appeared.

"...THE LIGHT IN THE SKY WAS SEEN BY MANY PEOPLE IN NORTHERN ENGLAND AND SOUTHERN SCOTLAND. A SPOKESMAN FOR THE ROYAL OBSERVATORY IN EDINBURGH SAID IT CERTAINLY WAS NOT A SHOOTING STAR OR METEOR. SOME EXPERTS BELIEVE THAT IT COULD WELL HAVE BEEN DEBRIS FROM THE RUSSIAN OR AMERICAN SPACE PROGRAMS, BURNING UP AS IT REENTERED THE ATMOSPHERE..."

Alex and Jim exchanged quick looks. There was a commercial break advertising washing powder. Mrs. Hood passed the cake around. Alex helped himself to a large slice. She looked up at the clock on the mantelpiece. "Goodness me, time's wearing on. The church service will be starting in less than an hour." She turned to Alex, "Would you like to come, Alex?"

Alex nodded, "Sure."

The phone rang out in the hall. Mrs. Hood jumped to her feet, "This might be Dad," and rushed out of the room, closing the door behind her. Alex and Jim each helped themselves to another wedge of cake. A few minutes later, she reentered the living room.

"Dad?" asked Jim

Mrs. Hood shook her head, "It was Mr. Dickson. Something unusual seems to have happened..."

Jim coughed as he choked on piece of cake and had to clear it with a swig of tea. Alex knew what Jim was thinking. The stranger had been found.

"What happened, Mrs. Hood?" asked Alex.

"It's Fiona. They got some bad news earlier tonight from Dr. Bruce. They went into the church to pray and when they got back, they found Fiona out of bed. She was very flushed. Earlier on she seemed to have been having hallucinations. They drove her to the hospital emergency and Dr. Bruce met them there. They just brought Fiona home. All the hospital doctors are baffled."

"What do you mean?" said Jim.

"They did some more tests. This time, they came up negative. The chronic condition they found before seems to have gone. Completely gone."

CHAPTER 6

NEWBATTLE CHURCH HAD BEEN IN existence for over two centuries. In that time, there had been special services bringing the community together at times of national peril, such as World War I and World War II. Those services were held in a spirit of unity and common purpose, but this one was different. Alex sat down with Jim and his mother in their usual pew, three rows from the back. He had never seen so many people at a church service, but there was tension in the air. A thin, horsehair stuffed, cushion pad provided nominal relief from the bum numbing effect of the hard wooden benches. By design, it fell short of providing enough comfort to encourage the pew dwellers to nod off during the sermon. Alex wriggled about for a moment in a futile attempt to mold the lumpy cushion into some conformity with his posterior. Even worse, the seat cushion felt slightly damp. Mrs. Hood ran her fingers along the wooden rail of the pew in front of her. "This is wet..." She pulled out a handkerchief and wiped the moisture from her hand.

Stuart Dickson, already seated in his high pulpit, viewed the congregation. In the front row, Fiona sat with her mother. She had given the boys a knowing smile when they had passed her. She looked well. Several low-key conversations blended into a steady buzz that reverberated off the marble covered walls.

Silence fell as Mr. Dickson stood up and placed his hands on the lectern, "My dear friends, let me first apologize for the damp conditions in the church. We appear to have a condensation problem in the building tonight." He grinned broadly. "I suggest the best way to eradicate this is to dry out the atmosphere with some enthusiastic praise. Let us worship the Lord by singing hymn number 172 in the church hymnary, 'O Little Town of Bethlehem.'" He let his eyes range over the congregation. "The industrial unrest of the past months continues to divide families and friendships." There was an outbreak of throat clearing and shuffling feet. The minister picked up his hymn book. "Let us listen to the words and pray that the everlasting light of love will drive out the darkness and division that haunts our streets."

The organist played the opening chords and the congregation began to sing in a somewhat tentative and subdued way. By the third verse, inhibitions fell away and the hymn ended with gusto.

Mr. Dickson held up both hands. "As many of you regular attendees know, our daughter, Fiona, has been the focus of our prayers for the last few weeks. We believe that we have experienced a Christmas miracle. She is able to be with us tonight because, according to the specialists at the hospital, she is completely free of the rare blood disease she has been battling against for some time." His last words were followed by some scattered applause and an excited buzz of conversations as he took out his handkerchief to blow his nose. He leaned both hands on the pulpit rail and let his eyes rove over the congregation. "Rose and I have already thanked the Lord for His healing of Fiona. Later, we will have communion open to all who wish to participate. Now, at the beginning of this special service, I would like us to pray for His healing touch on the cancer of mistrust and anger that is presently destroying the fabric of our village and nation." There followed some coughing and more shuffling of feet.

Alex lowered his head but did not close his eyes. His mind was still in some turmoil with the events of the day. He was aware of the steady breathing of the people around him. A cold draft of air swirled the dust on the floor around his feet. Someone had opened the vestry door at the rear of the sanctuary. Then came the sound of hesitant, shuffling, footsteps coming down the aisle behind him. Alex glanced to the side. He saw the frayed hem of an army overcoat. Slowly, he raised his eyes and a shiver ran up his spine. It was Sus. He was chewing something. In one hand was a partially eaten loaf of communion bread and in the other, an open bottle of communion wine. Then he saw Alex and his eyes lit up. He took a sudden step forward. Some liquid slopped out and splashed on the floor. Alex started to rise to his feet. A shrill cry rent the air. An elderly woman, three rows away, jumped to her feet, pointed a shaking finger at the stranger. "Drunk! Drunk!" Heads turned toward the disturbance. Sus's eyes stayed fixed on Alex. He took a half step forward.

Mr. Dickson started down the pulpit steps. Before he reached the floor, several men jumped from their seats to lay hold of the intruder. Bedlam reigned for the next few minutes. The minister managed to elbow his way through to Sus. "Outside!" he shouted. "Get him outside before someone gets hurt." He put his hands on Sus's shoulders and pushed him toward the vestry door. Bodies jammed together in the narrow aisle. Some overzealous assistance from one burly man at the rear sent the minister, Sus, and several others sprawling in an undignified heap on the vestry floor. The organist pushed her spectacles back up on the bridge of her nose and turned to her keyboard. Pulling out all the stops, she began a rousing rendition of "God Rest Ye Merry Gentlemen," adding to the bedlam of sound that filled the sanctuary.

There was a tug at Alex's sleeve. It was Fiona. A blue light flickered across the marble walls of the sanctuary. Fiona groaned. "It's the police."

Alex looked around. Mrs. Hood was on the other side of the sanctuary helping to calm some older ladies. "Let's go outside and see what's happening. Is there another way out?"

Jim nodded. "There is a side door behind the organ. Follow me." He slipped along the pew, followed by Alex and Fiona. The organist was oblivious to them as they passed behind her. The organ blared out above the chaos. This was, without doubt, one of her finest hours.

As they slipped out into the chill night air, they heard voices coming from around the rear of the church. The flickering blue light of the police car swept to and fro across the snow- covered trees. Alex started to inch his way along the sidewall to the corner of the building with the others close behind. He took a cautious peek. Two policemen stood with Sus held tight between them. One was Sergeant Brown, father of P.C. Brown. He was talking to Mr. Dickson and a group of elders. "We just got word that things are heating up down at the pit gates. Is there anywhere you can keep this man locked up till we get back?"

Mr. Dickson shook his head. "I don't think so, Sergeant." There was a burst of communication from the car radio. The other policeman let go of the stranger and stuck his head inside the car.

The sergeant shook his head. "I suppose we will have to take him in. It's been some night, Mr. Dickson."

The other policeman at the car called out, "Bad news, Sarge. Things got a bit rough down at the pit gates. They started to throw rocks..." He hesitated. "Bill's injured." The expression on the sergeant's face froze in the flickering blue light. He pushed Sus into the rear seat and slammed the door behind him. He scrambled into the front seat. The other policeman was already behind the wheel. The spinning tires sprayed up snow and gravel as the police car skidded out onto the highway, siren screaming, and raced off into the darkness. The minister and the other men disappeared into the church. The three youngsters huddled against the cold stone wall of the church."What do we do now?" said Jim glumly.

"I wish we could follow and see what they do to him," said Alex.

"There is the path down through the wood," said Fiona. "It goes all the way to the pit gates. In the days before everybody got cars, the miners used it as a shortcut."

Alex sighed, "I wish I had my sled."

"You can use mine," said Fiona. "It's a Flexible Flyer."

"Flexible Flyer?" scoffed Jim.

Fiona flashed him an irritated look, "My granny bought it at Jenners in Edinburgh. It was made in America. It's not just scrap wood nailed together like your junky sled."

Jim rolled his eyes. "Excuse me for living."

Fiona quickly turned toward Alex. "What do you think?"

As her earnest dark eyes met his, Alex shrugged. "I suppose it's worth a try."

"You'll go then?" she said.

Alex hesitated for a moment. "Sure," he finally said.

Fiona gave him a quick smile and ran off through the gate

into the back garden of the manse. Alex and Jim followed. Fiona's sled was leaning against tool shed. She laid it down on its metal runners. "You steer with the wooden crosspiece. If you lay down, you don't need to use your feet to steer so it is easier and a lot faster."

"Fiona! Where are you?" Mrs. Dickson's shrill sounding voice came from the church.

"I'm here Mum. I'm coming." She gently squeezed Alex's arm. "You better get going."

Alex felt the blood rush to his cheeks and was grateful for the darkness. "Okay. I'll see you in a bit." He set off at a run toward the bottom of the garden, dragging the sled. A gate gave access out into the open field that lay behind the manse. Soon, he reached the outer fringe of the wood. He found the path, a slash of white through the darkness. He pulled his gloves tighter, leaned his hands on the sled's rear and slid it back and forward for a few seconds. Taking a deep breath, he pushed off with several strong thrusts from his legs before launching himself onto the wooden slats that formed the top of the sled. His hands grasped the steering bar as the flyer accelerated down the slope.

The runners hissed through the icy snow. A bend appeared ahead. He tugged at the steering bar and the sled swept gracefully around the turn, throwing up a fantail of powdered snow behind it. He made another sweeping negotiation of the next bend. The path soon became less steep and, suddenly, he broke clear of the trees. The bright lights of the coalmine lit up the night. The stationary giant winding wheels on top of the pithead frame were now visible. The sled began to slow down and he slid to a halt at a bank overlooking the road and the main entrance gates to the colliery. Floodlights picked out a milling crowd. A police whistle pierced the night. Angry voices floated up toward him.

Halfcrouching, Alex made his way to the lip of the slope, pulling the sled behind him. A line of policemen in riot gear were driving back a crowd of placard-waving picketers. Stones and rocks rattled on the shields and the ground. Near the gate was the police car, doors wide open. Sergeant Brown was kneeling beside a prostrate figure in police uniform.

"Where's the blooming ambulance?" The tone in the sergeant's voice was a combination of anger and fear.

"It should be here soon, Sarge," somebody responded.

"Bill's bleeding to death. He'll be gone before they get here." He took hold of his injured son's shoulders. "Give me a hand; let's get him in the back of the car." The other constable jumped out from behind the driving wheel and they carefully lifted the limp figure and awkwardly slid him into the rear seat.

"I think we need to lay him out flat, Sarge. It's a bit tight with this other guy in there."

"I'll soon sort that." The sergeant ran around to the other side of the car and pulled open the rear door. "Out, my lad." He hauled Sus clear of the car and let him fall to the ground. Doors slammed. The car roared off down the road, followed by a hail of stones and jeers from the pickets. Alex watched the flashing blue lights disappear. Shouting drew his attention back to the pit gates. Now that their injured colleague was clear, the police were beating a rear guard action back through the pit gates with the picketers pressing hard. The last policeman squeezed through. The gates crashed shut as a hail of stones and broken placards bounced off the wire mesh. Sus had risen to his feet. One of the picketers stepped away from the melee and looked toward him. He took several steps and then stopped. He and Sus stared at each other in silence, oblivious to the riot going on around the gates. The picketer pointed a gloved hand at Sus. He spoke some words that were lost to Alex in the uproar. Sus, closer to Alex, responded in a clear voice. "Why are you here, servant of Tan?"

The picketer seemed to freeze at the words. He took a step back, then whirled around toward the crowd at the gate. "There's one of them lads!" He pointed at Sus. "It's one of their plain clothes gits..." With whoops of anger the large group of picketers broke away from the gates and ran screaming toward Sus.

CHAPTER 7

SUS RECOGNIZED THE DANGER AND started to run, rather awkwardly, down the road. The mob, in full cry behind him, was gaining fast. Without stopping to think, Alex grabbed the rear of the sled, pushed it to the lip of the slope, and threw himself on top. It raced diagonally down the slope and streaked onto the ice-covered roadway. Up ahead, the pickets were within yards of the fleeing Sus, baying like hounds as they closed the gap. The sled ploughed into the middle of the mob of pickets, clipped the ankle of one of the men, sending him crashing to the ground. A hail of curses sounded behind Alex as he pulled away from the mob. A flurry of stones whizzed overhead and rattled and bounced on the road around him. He took a quick glance over his shoulder. Several men were sprawled on the ground. The rest were still in hot pursuit. He drew alongside Sus, and dug in his toes to slow down.

"Jump on my back! Jump!" he shouted, jabbing his thumb over his shoulder. Sus threw himself on top of Alex. The sled lurched forward under the extra weight. The shouting faded as the road became steeper. As the sled's speed increased, Alex breathed easier. The mob would never catch them now.

A beam of light lit up the road in front of the sled. Alex jerked his head around. Two headlights pierced the darkness behind. A car had overtaken the running picketers. The car horn blared out above the crackling hiss of the sled's runners. Alex looked to right and left. Steep slopes on both sides. The roar of the car engine increased. Alex steered to the right side of the roadway. A bend was coming up. His only chance was to take the corner sharp and steal a few yards on the car. He swerved around the bend. The sled skidded. Flashing lights appeared dead ahead. A siren screamed out. Alex hauled the bar hard right. The sled left the road and raced up the bank and lost contact with the ground. The sound of squealing brakes and the crunch of metal against metal filled the air.

Alex landed heavily on his back. Winded, he lay for some time trying to suck air into his lungs. Someone leaned over him. "Are you well, Alex?" It was the soft voice of Sus.

Alex struggled to his feet, dusting the snow from his clothes. "I'm fine." He looked at Sus's face, illuminated in the cold light of the moon. "How about you?"

"I am fine also, Alex." Angry voices rose up from the roadway below.

Alex scrambled up the bank and took a cautious glance over the edge. A car lay on its side in the middle of the road. Its wheels were still spinning. An ambulance, red lights flickering, was nosed into the banking. The medics were hauling people out of the car. Judging by the heated exchange of words, there were no serious injuries on either side. Other pickets were running down the road toward the scene of the accident. Alex slipped back down the slope to rejoin Sus. "We better get away from here."

"Where shall we go, Alex?"

"To my house, I suppose."

"Let us go quickly!" Sus shivered as he spoke. He suddenly looked very tired.

Alex grabbed up the sled's towrope. "Stay close to me." He strode up the hill toward the tree line, dragging the sled. Sus followed close behind. He took a route that kept them clear of the village streets as much as possible. Some picketers might still be roaming around. Sus seemed more and more exhausted. At last they reached the back door of Alex's home. He leaned the sled against the wall, lifted the lid on the coal box, and picked out the spare back door key from its hideaway nail. As they stepped into the kitchen, they were met by a welcome draft of warm air as it rushed past them into the chill night. Alex ushered Sus in and quickly shut the door. He pulled his sodden gloves off and threw them onto a wooden chair and unzipped his anorak. "Would you like a cup of tea, Sus?"

Sus raised his eyebrows. "Tea?"

"It's a hot drink. It will warm you up."

Sus nodded, "That would be good."

Alex filled up the electric kettle and plugged it in. Sus watched his every action with great interest. Alex pulled off his anorak and hung it on a hook on the door. "I need to go to the bathroom. I'll be back in a minute."

"Bathroom? What is bathroom?" Sus raised his eyebrows.

Alex felt his ears warm up. "It's just something I have to do." He left the kitchen quickly. When he returned, Sus was staring at the whistling kettle. Alex was conscious of Sus watching his every move as he went through the ritual of tea making. He got Sus to sit down at the table and placed a steaming mug in front of him. "Help yourself to sugar and milk." Alex pushed the bowl and the jug toward Sus who looked puzzled. Alex, in spite of the tension he felt, laughed.

"Let me show you what to do." He spooned a generous spoonful of sugar into the mug, simultaneously pouring in milk. He stirred the spoon around a few times and slid the mug toward Sus.

Sus raised the mug to his lips and took a cautious sip. He swallowed and nodded his head. "Tea is good." He took another more generous sip.

"Would you like something to eat?" asked Alex.

Sus put down the mug, "To eat?"

Alex pointed to his mouth. "Food…Food to eat."

Sus nodded. "Food would be good."

Alex soon prepared a cheese sandwich, which Sus, after a tentative start, consumed with some gusto. Alex poured himself a mug of tea and sat down at the table. Sus was leaning back in his chair. He still looked far from well. His eyes once more appeared to be focused into the distance. "Are you feeling alright, Mr. Sus?"

"I feel strangely weak." Sus ran the fingers of both hands through his hair. He looked at Alex with a serious expression. "I must communicate with your leaders. I was supposed to land near London. I do not understand what has gone wrong."

"You can speak to them on the phone," Alex pointed to the telephone on the wall.

Sus shook his head. "That will not do. I must see them face to face."

Alex swallowed hard. "It must be awfully serious then?"

"Your world is in great danger, but it would be wrong to frighten all of your people with the knowledge."

Alex spilled some tea as he put the mug down. "What do you mean, 'danger?'"

Sus took a long sip of his tea, his blue green eyes stayed

fixed on Alex. He slowly put the cup down. "Where did you say is the center of government for this place?"

"In Edinburgh. It is the capital of Scotland. There are government offices there."

"Is Edinburgh far from here?" asked Sus.

Alex shook his head. "It's just seven or eight miles." He looked at his wrist watch. "The last bus has gone and it is too far to walk in this weather."

"What other way is there?" asked Sus.

"Well we could call a taxi, I suppose."

"Taxi? What is taxi?"

"Well, it's a car with a driver that you pay to take you places." Alex gave an apologetic smile."I don't have enough money though. It would cost pounds."

"Do you have such a vehicle?"

Alex swallowed hard. "Well, my dad has a wee car but..."

"Can you work this vehicle?"

Alex gave a nervous laugh. "Dad let me have a go, but that was in a field. I'm too young to have a drivers' license."

Sus stood up, "Can most people drive in this place?"

"Most adults can," said Alex.

Sus nodded his head. "Then I will have that skill. Where is the vehicle?"

Alex felt butterflies in his stomach. "It's in a garage at the bottom of the garden, but my Dad will go off his rocker. I'm not so..."

"Alex, please understand. Your world is in great danger. If I succeed in my mission, you will be honored. If I fail then..."

Alex, his thoughts whirling, began to pace back and forth across the room. The alien's eyes followed him. Alex stopped and gave out a deep sigh. "Okay. Let's give it a try, but I need to phone Jim and let him know."

Jim answered the phone on the first ring. "Where are you? I was about to phone the police." He sounded slightly irritated.

"I'm here at home. Sus is with me, Jim. We are going to Edinburgh."

There was a moment of silence at the other end. "What for?"

"Sus says the world is in danger. He has to speak to government leaders. It seems really serious, Jim."

"How are you going to get there?" asked Jim.

"Dad's car."

There was a gasp from the other end. "Are you nuts? You can't drive."

"Sus says he can," said Alex.

"But he's an alien. What about insurance?" Jim spluttered.

"Dad has comprehensive coverage."

"You're joking?"

"What else can I do, Jim? Sus says we will all be in big trouble if he fails to do what he's come here for." He cleared his throat. "Did you tell your mum about Sus?"

"No…she's still not back from church. She had to take a couple of the old wifies home. They were all worked up about the trouble at the church. I didn't get a chance to speak to her."

"What about Fiona? Did she speak to her mum and dad?"

Jim sighed. "She did. They think she has still got some fever. They made her go to bed."

Alex turned to look at Sus. "We have to go, Jim. I will phone you when I we get to Edinburgh."

"What am I going to tell my mum?"

"Think of something, Jim. I have to go," Alex hung up quickly.

Five minutes later, Alex and Sus were sitting in Mr. Watts's Morris Minor, inside the rather ramshackle shed that served as a garage. Sus was behind the wheel studying the controls. He turned to Alex.

"Does this vehicle have a manual?"

Alex pulled open the glove compartment and handed the tattered owner's book to Sus. Sus flicked quickly through the pages and then handed it back to Alex. "You have the key?"

Alex pointed, "It's already in the ignition."

Sus turned the key and the engine burst into life. He smiled and turned to Alex. "Are you ready?"

Alex forced a nervous smile, "I think so." The engine revs increased as Sus pushed down the clutch and slipped the stick into first gear. The car rolled out of the garage onto the access road. Alex directed Sus toward the main road through deserted back streets. Sus stared straight ahead, his features expressionless in the soft green light of the instrument panel. They drove out of the village. The road's surface sparkled with evening frost. Alex watched the alien out of the corner of his eyes. There was no doubt that he had mastered the basics of driving. He also seemed to be enjoying the experience. More so than Alex.

Sus turned and smiled. "This vehicle is good."

Alex shrugged. "It's okay. Mum wants to get a new one. Dad says they don't make them like this anymore."

Sus laughed softly, "It is the same where I come from." The roadway was clear of snow, but sparkled with the evening frost. The car passed over a crest in the roadway and there below them was the dark mass of the lowland plain. The lacework of lights that marked out the network of roads and communities spread out like a giant web. At the center of the web was the floodlit castle, floating regally above the ancient capital city of Edinburgh, like a giant stone spider guarding its territory. "Beautiful. Very beautiful," Sus said quietly.

"It's my dad's favorite view," said Alex.

"I can understand why. I..." Sus's voice trailed off.

Alex turned; the alien was staring straight ahead.

Alex glanced at the speedometer. 55...57...60...62. "You better slow up, Sus. The road looks slippy." 65...67...69...Sus did not respond. 71...73. Alex swallowed hard. The car started to weave. "Take it easy, Sus, or we..." Alex's warning died in his throat. Sus slumped across the steering wheel. The car swerved toward the center of the road. Alex grabbed at the wheel to steer them back to the left lane. He over corrected. The car ran off onto the snow covered verge for several yards. Metal crunched as the right front wing scraped along the low dry stone wall. The car dropped back down on to the roadway. Alex yelped in pain as the jolt caused him to bite his tongue. The salty warm taste of blood filled his mouth. The alien's limp body fell over onto him. The car started to drift across the roadway. Alex tugged the wheel. The car drifted to the left. He stretched out his right leg to reach the brake pedal. He couldn't get past the aliens legs. 75...77...80... His right hand closed around the hand brake. A red, triangular hazard warning sign loomed ahead. SHARP BEND. He shoved his shoulder against Sus's limp body. Steering with his left hand, he began to pull up on the hand brake. The car seemed to slow up a fraction. The curve of the stone wall up ahead marked the approaching bend. He hauled the brake up hard. The wheels locked and the car skidded in a straight line for several yards. He tried to steer into the curve. The wall raced toward them. Alex let go of the wheel and threw his arm across his face.

CHAPTER 8

ALEX SLOWLY OPENED HIS EYES. His head throbbed painfully. He put up his hand to push back his hair. Something wet and sticky adhered to his fingers. The engine was silent. The car sat sloped slightly to one side. Its headlights beamed aimlessly into the night sky. He quickly switched them off. He reached up and adjusted the rear view mirror. A narrow drip of blood ran down the side of his face. He gingerly ran his fingers through his hair. It was only a small cut. Then he remembered Sus. The alien was slumped back in the seat. His breathing was very shallow. "Sus? Sus? Are you Okay?" There was no response. Alex leaned over to look closely at the alien's face. The skin color was pale, almost grey. He pulled the door handle. Shivering as the chill air flowed into the car, he stepped out and slipped on frozen furrows. Pieces of broken wood were littered around the car. He looked back across the field. There was a space, like a missing tooth, in the grey line of the wall. The shattered remains of the gate hung from its posts. A few yards either way and the car and its occupants would have been a tangled mass. He turned to inspect the car. It did not appear to have suffered any major body damage. He opened the passenger door and leaned inside. Sus was flopped across the seat like a rag doll. Alex locked his arms around the alien and pulled him clear of the driver's seat. He propped the limp body up in the passenger seat and slid in behind the steering wheel. His one and only experience driving had been in a large empty car park with his brother beside him. He turned the ignition and the car lurched forward. After two false starts, the engine burst into life. He slipped the gear stick into first and raised his left foot slowly off the clutch. The car bounced its way over the frozen furrows toward the gateway. He gingerly maneuvered through the broken gate and stopped short of the road surface. He looked up and down the highway. There was no sign of traffic. He eased the stick into first and slowly released the clutch. The car rolled onto the road.

He turned toward the village and eased into second. His foot slipped on the clutch and the Morris jerked forward and went into a mild skid. Headlights appeared up ahead. He crouched down in the seat. The approaching driver flashed his high beam and honked its horn. Alex almost jumped out of his seat. The other car raced past, its horn still blaring. He had forgotten to switch on his lights. His trembling fingers fumbled in the darkness to locate the light switch. He clicked it on and the twin beams carved out the darkness ahead of him.

The journey home only took fifteen minutes, but seemed to take an eternity. The car skidded several times. His insides churned every time another car passed, but at last he made it to the lane that led to the rear of his house. Alex let out a gasp of relief as he steered through the still open garage doors and brought the car to a halt. He quickly turned off the ignition and the headlights. He sat for a few moments, feeling a brief sense of security in the darkness. Sus groaned but remained slumped in the passenger seat. Alex opened the door and stepped out. The cold air chilled the sweat that beaded on his forehead. He pulled out his handkerchief and mopped his face. He looked at the still form inside the car. There was no way he could get Sus into the house on his own. He had to get help. He quietly closed the car door and ran down the path to the back door. Once inside, he phoned Jim.

Jim's mother still had not returned and, ten minutes later, Jim had arrived and helped carry Sus into the house. They laid him down on the settee in the kitchen. Alex brought a blanket from his bedroom and carefully spread it over Sus. Alex got two cans of Irn-Bru from the fridge and sat down at the kitchen table with Jim. Between sips, Alex rested the can firmly on the table top to steady his nervous hands.

"We should call Dr. Bruce," said Jim.

"He won't come. He thinks Sus is just a drunk. We need to find someone who believes us." He took another sip.

Jim sighed. "Right, that's all we need. Somebody who believes in flying saucers and wee green men."

Alex banged down his can, spilling some liquid on the table, "That's it! Why didn't we think of that before?"

"What are you blethering about?"

"Mr. McCracken. The man in the old quarry cottage. The UFO investigator."

"The man is a weirdo," protested Jim. "Remember when he said he saw aliens up at the Gladhouse reservoir fishing? He said he knew they were aliens because they didn't have any fishing line on their rods. The guy's a 'fruit and nut' case."

"That's just it," said Alex. "Our story sounds pretty crazy. Maybe he's not nuts. Maybe he is for real."

Jim shook his head, "Och away with you...remember

all that business about the crop circles in farmer Wallace's fields?"

"I went to see some of them," said Alex. "The wheat was flattened down in a perfect circle. There were scientists there from Edinburgh University doing all sorts of tests."

"Yes," scoffed Jim. "Until that night somebody saw two guys stamping out a circle with their feet and planks of wood."

"That was only one time and they never caught them," said Alex.

Jim shook his head. "My mum knows the person who saw them and he swore that McCracken was one of them." He took a sip of Irn-Bru. "Anyway, the scientist people quit nosing around after that."

"We tried to tell the police what we have seen tonight and where did that get us? McCracken might be for real. He may not be as crazy as we all thought."

"I suppose so," said Jim grudgingly.

"Well, let's go and talk to him," said Alex.

"Now?" gasped Jim. "Mum will be wondering where we are." He looked toward the blanket covered figure on the settee."What about him? Can we just leave him here?"

Alex sighed. "I suppose so. It will only take half an hour at the most. We can take Fiona's sled for coming back. We will come back in no time."

Ten minutes later, they were heading out of the village, trudging up the narrow country road that circled around the lower slopes of Jake's Law. Alex was in front dragging Fiona's sled. He kept his head down. An icy breeze blew powdered snow from the hedgerows into his eyes. He raised his head, blinking through the stinging hail. Up ahead, a yellow blob of light broke the darkness. He could make out the dark shape of Mr. McCracken's isolated cottage.

"He's in anyway," said Alex.

"Terrific!" said Jim, wiping the melting snow from his face, "Maybe he'll have hot cocoa and a plate of digestive biscuits waiting for us." As they neared the cottage, they could hear a TV blaring above the gusting wind. A pile of cylindrical objects were stacked up against the end wall of the cottage. Jim brushed some of the snow off the stack and picked up one of the cylinders. It was about six inches in diameter. He rubbed it with his gloved hand. "It's not concrete. It's stone, like they get out of boreholes."

Alex nodded. "Old McCracken's some sort of geologist. He put an advert in the *Dalkeith Advertiser* when he first came here asking folk to bring any unusual rocks to him for his research."

Jim nodded. "He said he would pay five bob for every sample he kept. He was particularity interested in cylindrical shape rocks. He must have run out of money quick. There were hundreds of these rock samples people had found up at the Roman Camp Woods where the opencast coalmine used to be. The Coal Board did a lot of test bores around there. My dad has one. He uses it to sharpen knives."

Alex's thoughts returned to the task in hand. He walked around to the front of the cottage. The curtains were all closed. Displayed in the front widow was a printed cardboard sign: "UFO INVESTIGATOR."

Chapter 9

J IM POINTED TO THE SIGN. "We've come to the right place anyway."

Alex took a deep breath and pressed the door bell. Westminster chimes echoed from behind the door. There was the sound of a chair moving. The TV went off and footsteps were coming toward them. The door opened quickly. Alex blinked as the hall light spilled out into the night. Framed in the doorway was the dark shape of a tall man. "Well, good evening lads. What are you two doing out on a night like this?" The voice was soft and friendly.

Alex stepped forward brushing his hair back from his eyes. "We're sorry to bother you at this time of night, Mr. McCracken, but we needed to speak to you."

Jim spoke up. "We've seen a UFO."

"Whereabouts?" McCracken's tone was sharper.

Alex answered. "On the top of Jake's Law. It came right down out of the sky and it brought a wee man with it."

The door opened wider. "You better come in and tell me the whole story." McCracken stepped back, ushering them into the warm living room. McCracken was wearing thin, leather gloves. He was a tall man, rather thin, with an untidy mop of grey hair and a small moustache. He wore round metal framed glasses and a shapeless Harris Tweed suit. He waved them toward a settee set to one side of a blazing coal fire and sat himself down in the overstuffed leather armchair opposite. Alex looked around the room. The walls were covered with framed photographs of UFOs. He sneezed and quickly pulled out his handkerchief. McCracken took a briar pipe out of his pocket and stuck it into his mouth. He took a box of matches and lit up. After a few puffs he settled back into his seat. He smiled. "Well lads, tell me all about what happened. Everything you saw and heard. Don't worry; you have come to the right place." Alex's eyes strayed to McCracken's hands. McCracken smiled, "Please excuse these gloves. I have a skin condition, which I am trying to clear up. Now let's hear your story and please do not leave out any details, regardless of how trivial they may seem to you."

Alex launched into a description of the events of the evening. McCracken listened intently, puffing away steadily. He made few interruptions, mostly to confirm the names of the people. But when Alex said Sus's name, McCracken seemed most attentive.

"Sus you say?" He took his pipe out of his mouth and leaned forward. "Are you sure that was the name?"

"Yes," said Alex. "Does that mean anything?"

McCracken smiled. "No!" He settled back in his chair, "It's not often that alien visitors give names, that's all." He waved his hand. "Carry on, Alex. Finish your story please."

Alex went on to complete his account. McCracken had closed his eyes.

"Do you believe us, Mr. McCracken?" asked Jim.

McCracken's eyes widened, "Of course, my boy, of course." He stood up and knocked his pipe out on the fireplace grate and jammed it back into his coat pocket. He turned to face them. "So this Sus is at your house, Alex? What about your parents?"

"They aren't supposed to return until tomorrow. They are at a meeting in Edinburgh."

"I see." McCracken stroked his chin as he spoke. He started to pace the floor, followed by two pairs of eyes. Then he slumped back down into the chair, rubbing his gloved hands. "We have a problem, lads. We have great forces opposing us."

"Aliens?" asked Jim.

"Not just aliens, my lad. It's our government who will work against us, as they have against me for the past two years."

"Maybe they are worried that people would panic," said Alex.

"No...it's nothing to do with that. It's oil that's the problem...oil." McCracken appeared irritated.

"But what has oil to do with UFOs? They surely don't use oil," said Jim.

McCracken pounded the arms of the chair with his gloved hands. "Exactly, they don't use oil. If it became known to the general public that a craft already exists that can use a power source that is not based on oil, imagine the tremendous pressure on government to develop similar sources of power. Once that was achieved, what would happen to the oil business?" He paused, but before they could respond he answered his own question. "Collapse. Complete collapse of all the big oil companies. And the financial empires connected with them. At present, they control the whole world. The Americans and the Russians are in this as well, pawns of the oil cartels."

Alex shook his head, "But surely the government would want to defend us against an invasion by aliens?"

"That's just it," said McCracken. "They believe that these alien visitors are friendly and mean no harm. It's a calculated risk. They will strive to keep oil as the main power source until it starts to dry up. Then they will open up their safes and produce alternative sources of energy which they will control." McCracken jumped to his feet. "But enough of this, boys. We have work to do, to keep our alien friend out of the clutches of the government people, and get him to some honest opposition member of parliament who will listen to his story." He jumped to his feet. "Where is your house, Alex?"

"McLean Place," said Alex. "30 McLean Place."

McCracken nodded his head. "I know where you are." He rubbed his chin for a few seconds. "Look boys, I think I should contact some friends of mine who can help us. One is a doctor. It sounds like our visitor needs some medical attention." He paced over to the window and drew back the curtain. "It's stopped snowing thank goodness." He turned to them. "If you just wait here while I phone."

Jim stood up quickly. "I can't wait, Mr. McCracken. My mum will be worried."

Alex also stood up. "I need to get back. Sus may come round. He will wonder where I am."

McCracken looked slightly annoyed. He gave a forced smile, "I can run you home in my Volkswagen."

Jim shook his head, "We have a sled. It's too big to get in your car."

Alex nodded his head. "He's right, Mr. McCracken. We have to take it back to the person who it belongs to. It's downhill all the way. We will be home in a few minutes. I will wait for you at my house."

McCracken's smile returned. "Of course." He slapped his gloved hands together. "We will meet at your place in about thirty minutes or so. Remember, we cannot afford to share this with anyone, not even your parents. If this story leaks out to the wrong people, Sus will be in extreme danger. You understand?"

"Yes, we understand," said Alex. McCracken escorted them to the front door. The chill air swept through the open door, but the snow had stopped falling and stars glittered in the clear night sky once more. Alex stepped out onto the frozen ground. Jim was right behind and quickly pushed past and headed for the sled. Alex turned to McCracken. "Thanks for your help, Mr. McCracken."

McCracken, whose dark shape was framed in the doorway, nodded curtly. "Don't mention it lad, but remember we must keep a lid on this." He smiled. "I must get on with my phone calls. I will see you shortly." He went back into the cottage closing the door behind him.

Alex pulled up the zipper on his anorak as he walked toward Jim who already was standing by the sled. "Did you ever hear such a load of cobblers. He has a slate missing off his roof. He's cuckoo."

"He at least listened to us, Jim. We need to give him a chance."

Jim sighed. "Let's get moving before we freeze to death."

Alex patted his pockets and groaned. "What's wrong now?" Jim spoke with some irritation.

"I've lost my inhaler," said Alex as he once more searched his pockets, to no avail.

"When did you last use it?" said Jim.

"Up on Jake's Law…when we were messing around in the snow." As he spoke, Alex realized that he hadn't had an asthma attack since then. It was surprising on a cold night like this and with all the excitement and physical activity. Then he remembered that he had pulled out his handkerchief when he and Jim were sitting on the settee in McCracken's living room. "Wait just a minute, Jim. I think it might have fallen out of my pocket when we were talking to old McCracken." He started to head back to the front door and Jim, with a martyred groan, pulled up his collar and sat back onto the sled.

There was no response to the doorbell. The chimes echoed inside. Alex tried the door. It was open. He pushed the door slightly ajar. "Hello! Mr. McCracken...are you there?" There was no sound other than the tick tock of the old wall clock that was hanging in the entrance hall. Alex opened the door further and stepped inside. "Hello! Hello!" There was still no response. He cautiously entered the living room. There was no sign or sound of McCracken. Alex moved quickly to the settee. He couldn't see his inhaler. He bent over and ran his fingers behind the cushion he had been sitting on. His fingers touched something. He pulled up the cushion and there was his inhaler. With a sigh of relief, he grabbed it and placed it into one of his zipper pockets. Then he noticed something else peeking out from under one of the cushions. It was a small bronze medallion. He picked it up. On one side it had a colored enamel center piece with the image of a soccer player on it. He turned it. On the other side was engraved writing.

"Where are you?" Jim's voice came from the front door. Alex ran out of the room. Jim was kicking his feet against the door step. "What took you so long?"

Alex held out his open hand. "Is this football medal yours? I found it under the cushions."

Jim shook his head. "It's not mine."

"I better put it back."

"You can give it to old McCracken when he comes to your house. I'm freezing. Let's get moving." Alex stuck the medallion in his pocket. Jim was already heading toward the sled. Jim grabbed up the ropes and dragged it down onto the icy road. When they reached the beginning of the hill, Jim jumped onto the front and Alex clambered on behind him. Jim steered a straight course down the center of the narrow road. The runners rattled over the ice- packed surface. Alex ducked his head behind Jim's back to shelter himself from the chilling wind-stream. Just a few minutes later, they were coasting through the village and slid to a halt at the entrance to Alex's street. They scrambled to their feet. Jim looked at his watch. He groaned out loud, "I need to get home right now and we still need to take the sled back to Fiona."

Alex rubbed his face to bring back the circulation into his frozen cheeks. "Why don't you take it home now and phone her. Let her know what happened. We can give her the sled back tomorrow. I'll go to my place and wait for Mr. McCracken. He will take over then and I'll come to your place."

Jim looked doubtful. "My mother will be asking where you are."

Alex shrugged. "Tell her I had to go home to pick up my toothbrush, which is true anyway."

Five minutes later, Alex turned the key in his front door. He flicked the hall light switch, but no light came on. The bulb was blown. He moved slowly down the dark hall toward the closed kitchen door. A strip of light spilled out from below the bottom of the door. Alex took the handle and turned it slowly. He pushed the door slightly ajar. "Sus...Sus? Are you there?" No reply. All he heard was the sound of a dripping tap.

He took a deep breath and pushed the door all the way open. The first thing he saw was the empty couch. The blanket lay on the floor. He stepped cautiously into the kitchen. A cold draft of air hit his face. The back door was wide open. On the floor, just inside the doorway, a thin dusting of snow was melting on the floor.

CHAPTER 10

ALEX RAN TO THE BACK door. There were footprints in the thin dusting of snow on the back steps. They carried on down the path toward the back gate. He ran down to the gate. It was half open. The footprints continued on through into the darkness. He cupped his hands to his mouth. "Sus!... Sus! Where are you, Sus?" The only sound was the creaking of the snow- laden branches from the fir tree. The sound of a car door slamming was followed by the distant buzz of the front doorbell. Alex gave a sigh of relief and ran back into the house, slamming the back door closed behind him. He ran down the hall and pulled open the front door. McCracken stood there, clad in a heavy suede coat and Russian style fur hat. He stepped inside. "Sorry I took so long, Alex."

"He's gone! Mr. McCracken. Mr. Sus has gone."

"Gone? I thought he was ill?"

"He was when we left, but I've searched the house. I found his footprints out back." He went to a drawer and took out a small flashlight. "I am going to take another look outside."

McCracken nodded. "Okay! I need to get my flashlight from the car." He turned and walked quickly down the hall. Alex opened the back door and, flashlight in hand, headed

68

down the path toward the gate. The footprints crossed the back road and then headed off across the open field. They were irregular, weaving from side to side. There was a disturbed area, evidence of a fall. He traced them as far as the beam reached. They were heading for Jake's Law. A stiff breeze had sprung up and powdered snow swirled across the field like miniature white sand storms. The footprints would soon be gone. He turned to head back to the house. Something brushed against his face. He ducked away to one side, lashing out with his hand. He slipped and fell on his knees and the flashlight was jerked from his hand. He grabbed it back up and swung it round. Just outside the gate was a telephone pole. Something hung from it. A loose cable. The frayed end whipped to and fro in the breeze. The other end of the broken telephone cable lay partially buried in the snow alongside the path. He picked it up. More cable appeared. He gave it a jerk. A broken tree branch lifted clear of the snow. The cable was caught underneath it. The cable broke free from the branch and swung up into the air. His flashlight traced its rising path up to the connector on the back wall of the house.

"Alex?" McCracken's dark outline appeared framed in the back doorway.

"I'm here, Mr. McCracken." Alex walked quickly back to the house.

McCracken smiled as Alex stepped into the brightly lit kitchen. "I was getting worried for a minute there, lad. I thought you had taken off without us."

"The wind is springing up, Mr. McCracken. Sus's tracks will be gone before long." He brushed some snow off his jeans. "It's freezing as well. We should contact the police and get some help."

McCracken smiled. "Great minds think alike, Alex. When

you were outside I took the liberty of using your phone to call the police station. They should be here shortly." McCracken looked at his wristwatch. "My friends should also be here to help soon. I will go back out front to keep an eye out for them."

Alex struggled to keep his voice steady. "Okay." He walked over to the sink. "I'll put the kettle on for some tea." He picked up the kettle and glanced over his shoulder. McCracken had left the kitchen. Alex dumped the kettle down on the counter and ran over to the phone. He scooped it up. The line was dead. McCracken had lied. He shivered and sneezed. He pulled his handkerchief out of his pocket. Something rattled onto the vinyl floor. As he wiped his nose he knelt down and picked up the object. It was the small bronze medallion he had found at McCracken's cottage. He turned it over to read the engraved inscription.

East of Scotland Junior Champions 1956
Arniston Rangers F C
A. Blyth, Centre Forward

A cold sensation ran up his spine. He went over to the sideboard and picked up one the framed photograph of his dad's football team. A younger Mr. Watts was seated in the center of the front row holding a large silver cup in his hands. A small blackboard rested against his legs with bold chalk writing on it.

Arniston Rangers FC
1956 Scottish Champions

Sitting in the front row, next to his father, was the more youthful face of the Andy Blyth he had known, the village newsagent, his father's best friend. Andy Blyth, who had been missing for over a year. Who had left home one December night and had never returned. Thoughts raced feverishly through his head. McCracken had lied about the police. He might just want to keep them out of it. But what was his connection with Andy Blyth? He went to the back door and slowly opened it. He reached the gate and carefully pulled it open. He heard the muffled sound of an engine. A car was creeping down the back road heading toward him. The headlights were yellow. The previous summer the Watts Family had gone on a motoring tour of France. The French required all cars to have yellow headlights. His dad had purchased a conversion kit from the Automobile Association, which had included yellow plastic lens that clipped over the headlights. The car creeping down the lane had the same filters. This car had recently been in France. About fifty yards from his gate, the car stopped and the engine died. The lights went out. Alex ducked back from the gate. He looked back to the house. Then came the sound of car doors opening and shutting and the muffled crunch of stealthy footprints. They were approaching the gate. Alex felt his heart beating in his chest. He looked around. An alley between his house and the neighboring house giving access to the front street was his only option. Crouching low, Alex ran toward the alley entrance. Just then, he heard McCracken call out. "Alex! Are you there?"

He ran down to the end of the alley. McCracken's Volkswagon was parked outside his house but the street was deserted. Once more he heard McCracken calling. Another voice answered. Alex couldn't make out the words. One thing was for sure, McCracken was not what he seemed. He could be working for the government. Alex had to get to Sus before

McCracken and his associates did. Keeping close to the wall, he worked his way down the path until he came to another narrow opening between buildings.

Soon, he was crunching across the frozen field toward the massive cone shaped bulk of Jake's Law. He took out his flashlight and, using his body to shield it from the direction of the village, searched the snow ahead as he trudged diagonally up the lower slopes of the hill. It was not long before he came upon Sus's trail. There was no mistaking the small fresh footprints. He flicked off the flashlight and began trudging up the increasingly steep slope. He looked back toward the village. A small cluster of moving lights had appeared in the darkness of the open field that lay between his house and the foot of the hill. Others were following Sus's trail. They would soon find his. He climbed faster. He could still make out the trail of Sus's footprints without the aid of the flashlight. The higher he climbed, the more his feet sank into deeper snow. Breathing heavily, he looked back over his shoulder. The string of lights was much closer. He plunged on toward the summit.

At last, he stumbled over the lip and stood on the summit. He stood for some moments drawing air into his lungs. The breeze was stronger at the higher altitude. Whirling eddies of powdered snow swept across the surface of the law. He took a step forward, sheltering in the lee of one of the standing stones and cupped his hands to his mouth. "Sus...Sus? Are you there?" The wind swept away his words. There was a brief lull in the strength of the wind. Then he saw something. The dark outline of a figure standing close to the ruined walls of the chapel. Alex flicked on the flashlight and moved cautiously forward.

"Sus...is that you?"

"Yes, Alex. How did you find me?"

Alex moved up close. "I followed your footprints. There are other people coming up the hill, Sus. I think they are out to get you. We have to leave here."

"This was where you and Jim first met me, Alex?" Sus's voice sounded stronger than before.

"Yes! Don't you remember?"

"Was there a light? A blue beam of light?"

Alex nodded. "Yes, that happened first. It shot straight up like a searchlight from the center of the chapel. A big silver sphere spiraled down." He paused. "There was a weird gas cloud thing that fired laser beams at us."

Sus gave a rueful smile. "I'm afraid it was part of the process."

Alex felt a sinking feeling in his stomach. "Are you going to leave?"

"That was my plan, Alex, but there is a problem. Something is missing." He stepped through the stone arch doorway into the roofless interior of the chapel. Alex followed him. The floor of the chapel was paved with irregularly shaped flagstones. One, in the center, was completely shattered, its pieces scattered all over the floor, exposing an area of natural bedrock. At its center was a round hole. "There should have be a stone here in this cavity," said Sus.

"A stone?" Alex knelt down and aimed his flashlight into the hole. It was perfectly round, six inches or so in diameter, and twelve inches deep with smooth sides.

"A special stone, Alex. A trigstone. It was designed to fit in with the natural surroundings, but it has a device imbedded in it. The column of blue light that you saw was activated by the vehicle I travelled in. To bring the vehicle back, I have to activate the beam from here with the trigstone device."

Alex suddenly remembered McCracken. He ran across to the edge of the summit and looked down into the darkness below. "You need to look at this Sus. They are spreading out as they climb up. They will soon cut us off."

Sus walked over to join Alex. He studied the advancing lights in silence for some seconds. "I do not think these are your people, Alex. They are Tan's men. I may already be too late."

"Too late for what?"

Sus did not answer immediately. He raised his head skywards, then pointed straight up. "What do you call that, Alex?"

"You mean the Milky Way?"

Sus nodded. "I come from beyond what you see, from the other side of the galaxy. My home is the chief planet in the Outer Galactic Alliance and the leader of the Alliance is my father, President Vah. Tan was a member of the Alliance council." Sus turned to Alex. "He tried to undermine the democratic process to obtain more power and influence for himself. My father ejected him from the council. Some of the other council members chose to leave with Tan. An intergalactic civil war broke out between Tan's group of rebel planets and the Alliance." Sus looked up into the heavens. "The Alliance prevailed and Tan's forces were defeated. Tan was never found. We captured one of his generals and he told us that, before the final battle, Tan escaped with a small but powerful fleet of battle cruisers, which he planned to use to establish his regime on the other side of the galaxy."

"Where?" asked Alex.

"Here on Earth."

Alex felt a chill run up the back of his neck.

"Once he is firmly in control, he will use his base on

Earth to rebuild his forces and, sometime in the future, make another attempt to take control of the Alliance." Sus turned to watch the line of lights moving upward toward them.

"Is there nothing we can do?" said Alex quietly.

Sus shook his head. "Not at the stage of technical development on Earth. But that is why my father has sent me, to warn and to provide the technology to your leaders that would help them oppose Tan's invasion fleet."

"Why couldn't your father send his fleet after Tan?"

"Tan's fleet will reach Earth long before our fastest manned cruisers could catch up. He would have destroyed your civilization before we could stop him."

"How did you get here first?"

"The vehicle I arrived in was an untested prototype, one of a kind, capable of transporting one passenger across vast distances and space very quickly. For my body to withstand the journey, its molecular structure was loosened for the flight and then reestablished after I landed."

"The gas cloud and those light beams that hit Jim and I?"

"I'm afraid so, Alex. The information on the composition of your body, as well as Jim's and others in the vicinity, was necessary to reestablish my body in a form acceptable on this planet." He smiled. "I apologize for your discomfort during the process, and, though not harmful to you, it must have been frightening."

"You're not kidding, but it obviously worked. You even speak like one of us."

Sus nodded. "Yes, but I'm afraid this part of the process has not worked perfectly. It appears that the further I get away from this hill, the weaker I become."

"What could be wrong?"

Sus shook his head. "I'm not sure. The beacon is part of

the problem, but there is something else wrong. These lapses in and out of weakness do not make sense."

Alex looked down the hill. "They're getting awfully close Sus. We must leave now."

"You must go, Alex. I will stay."

Alex was stunned. "They will kill you!"

Sus shrugged his shoulders. " My mission has failed, Alex. I am unable to leave the village to make contact with your leaders. Tan's fleet will strike Earth long before my father's battle fleet arrives. Your planet will suffer considerable damage, loss of life, and trauma, but Tan will eventually be defeated. There will be survivors here on Earth and my desire is that you and your friends will be amongst those." Sus placed his hand on Alex's shoulder. "Here, close to the beacon, I have strength. If I go down to the village, I will become weaker and weaker and, in a few more hours, I shall be dead anyway. Here, I can die in an honorable manner worthy of a son of President Vah."

Alex straightened his back. "Then I will stay with you."

Sus sighed. " Please go, Alex."

"I will if you go with me." He paused for a moment. "Down in the village you will be weaker, but you won't be alone. If we can convince the police, they could contact the government and, though you can't go to them, they can come to you. It's worth a try Sus."

Sus looked at Alex, then down the hill. Alex pointed toward the advancing lights. "They haven't linked up yet. Over to the left there is still a gap we could get through."

"Then let us try," said Sus.

They set off around the edge of the summit toward the point above the gap between the two strings of lights. They were still some distance apart, but closing fast. Alex's heart sank. There was no way they could get down the slope fast enough. Sus had come to the same conclusion. He turned to look back across the summit of the law. "Could we get down on the other side of the hill?"

Alex shook his head. "The quarry face is over there. It will be dangerous."

Sus looked back down toward the advancing lights of their hunters. "We don't have much choice." Without further discussion they set off toward the far slope. They had only gone a few yards when they came upon a snow-covered pile of rubble. It was all that was left of a Observer Corp post from the second world war. Alex shone his flashlight on it. Amongst the bricks and broken concrete were pieces of rusty corrugated metal. Alex flicked off his flashlight and stuck it back into his pocket. He took hold of a piece and dragged it clear of the rubble heap. It was almost six feet long and curved up at one end. Though rusty, it was still quite rigid.

He turned to Sus. "We can use this to go down the hill."

Sus looked doubtful. "Can we control its direction?"

Alex shrugged. "Not very well, but it would go downhill." He dropped the section down and slid it back and forward on the snow. "It's pretty slippy."

Sus smiled. "I trust your judgment."

In spite of the cold, Alex's cheeks flushed. He slid the metal sheet back toward the rim of the slope. "We have to lay side by side holding on to the curved bit at the front."

"How do we direct its path?" said Sus.

"I will lay on the left side and you can go on the right." He lay down on the metal to demonstrate. "If we want to go left, I will dig my left foot in the snow, and if we need to go to the right, you will dig your right foot in."

Sus lay down beside Alex, holding on with both hands to

the curved front. "I think you should be the commander of this vehicle."

"Okay." Alex raised his head to look over the curved front. The lights were getting very close together. "Let's go." He pushed hard with his foot and the makeshift sled slipped over the edge and began to slide downhill.

CHAPTER 11

"**L**EFT!" A**LEX DUG HIS LEFT** toe into the snow. The metal sheet skidded clumsily to the left. They were sliding faster and faster. " Sus! Right!" Sus dug in his right foot. The corrugated metal bounced and flexed noisily as it skidded right. Alex raised his head above the lip of the curved metal. A string of lights was dead ahead and coming up fast. Alex ducked his head. There was a sickening thump and a figure hurtled overhead and crashed into the snow behind them. Alex strained his head to look behind. Flashlight beams swung erratically across the hillside. A pinpoint of blue light appeared in the blackness and streaked toward them. A chilling blast of cold air struck his face. A hole, the size of a saucer, had appeared in the curved metal front.

"Energy gun," shouted Sus. "Stay down!" Another blob of blue light streaked overhead. Alex squinted through the hole. A dark shape appeared dead ahead. It was a clump of small trees. Alex dug his toes hard into the snow. The metal sheet swerved sharply and tipped over. Alex landed on his shoulder and ploughed through the snow for several yards before coming to a halt. He sat up, wiping snow out of his eyes and ears. Sus was on his hands and knees a few yards away.

"Are you okay?" Alex called out.

"Yes..." Sus stood up. He looked back up hill. Alex followed his gaze. Several flashlight beams crisscrossed erratically over the hillside as their hunters scrambled down toward them. Alex spotted the corrugated sheet upside down amongst the small clump of trees. He looked down toward the village. A car was racing along the street; its yellow headlights bounced as it mounted the curb and headed across the open ground toward the foot of the hill. Alex groaned.

"That's the car that was at my house," Alex turned to Sus. "They have us trapped." He looked back up hill. The jerking flashlight beams were less than a hundred yards away.

"Get the metal sheet. Quickly!" The authority in Sus's voice caused Alex to obey immediately. He dragged the sheet back to Sus who began to dig snow with his hands and dump it onto the sheet. He turned to Alex. "We can send this downhill as a decoy. You understand?" Alex nodded his head and began to help heap snow onto the sheet.

In no time they had a sizable mound packed down. In a flash of inspiration, Alex took out his flashlight, flicked it on, and stuck it into the top of the mound of snow. They slid the sheet clear of the trees and launched it off on a diagonal route across the slopes. Slowly, it built up speed. Shouting broke out from behind them. Sus grabbed Alex's arm and pulled him toward the clump of trees. They buried themselves in the snow between the trees. The crunch of running feet was all around them. Alex pressed down deeper into the snow, holding his breath. The sounds started to fade. He raised his head slowly. He could still see the decoy light on the makeshift sled which was descending rapidly down the slope, its progress marked by pulsating balls of blue piercing the air around it.

Alex and Sus safely reached the outskirts of the village. The houses and street lights gave some feeling of security, but he knew it would not be long before McCracken discovered their ruse. He led Sus through deserted alleys and side streets. Sus was breathing heavily. The sound of a car engine came from behind. Alex turned and saw the yellow headlights! He grabbed Sus's arm and ran down another alley. He glanced over his shoulder. The car passed the alley entrance without slowing up. Alex let out his breath. They reached the end of the alley. He stopped and took a cautious glance into the street. It was deserted except for a small group of youths and parked motorbikes outside a brightly lit shop-front. The small, flashing sign above the door spelled out, "Video Games Café." A small string of multicolored lights above the doorway served to indicate the festive season.

Sus was shivering noticeably and his breathing had developed a wheeze.

"Are you alright?" Alex whispered.

"Yes...but cold."

Alex looked back at the café. He stuck his hand into his pocket and his fingers closed on a few coins. He pulled them out and peered at them in the dim light. Eighty-five pence, enough for a couple of coffees. With McCracken's gang prowling around, it would be wise to lay low for a bit.

"Come on, we can get something at the café," Alex led Sus across the street. The motorbike youths gave them a casual glance as they walked past. Alex pushed open the door. They were met by a mixed sound of disco music and the electronic chatter of video games. The café had two sections. One side had a jukebox and a few formica covered tables; the other had four rows of video games. Between the two sections was the small service counter with its steaming espresso coffee machine and a display case of stale looking sandwiches, pies, and assorted biscuits. Alex led Sus to a corner table. Four girls sat at the table next to them, deep in conversation interrupted by regular glances through the windows at the motorbike boys. Three younger boys were playing video games with the desperate intensity of zealots.

A door behind the counter opened and a small, stout grey haired woman appeared. A cigarette hung limply from her lips. She gave Alex and Sus a look that indicated there was no table service. Alex stood up and walked over to the counter.

"What will it be, sonny?" She forced a smile, brushing back a front lock of hair, tinted yellow by cigarette smoke. "We have some nice fresh meat pies."

"Just two coffees please, Mrs. Black," Alex pulled out his money.

The smile vanished. She clattered two cups, saucers, and spoons onto a scratched wooden tray and took it to the espresso machine. She reappeared from fresh clouds of steam with two overfilled cups of coffee and the cigarette still miraculously hanging from her lip. She banged the tray down, slopping the coffee into the saucers in the process. "Seventy pence. Sugar and milk at the table."

Alex handed over the money and carried the tray back to the table. Sus was watching the video game players with great interest. Alex set the cups down on the table and sat down. He picked up the sugar dispenser and offered it to Sus. Sus studied it for a few seconds then poured the white granules into the coffee. He did not halt till Alex held out his hand. "That should be enough, Sus." Sus handed the dispenser to Alex, but kept his eyes on the video game players. Alex looked up. The girls had stopped talking and were staring at Sus.

Alex stared back at them. The girls resumed their discussion about the motorbike boys.

Sus sipped the hot liquid, his eyes still fixed on the game players. Alex took a mouthful. The coffee was a better quality than the service, its warmth melting away the chill of the night. Sus put down his cup. "Tell me what has happened since we left to go to the city."

Alex quickly filled in the details of the events that had taken place. When he reached the part about McCracken, the UFO investigator, Sus's expression became grave. When Alex had finished, Sus went silent for some time. Then he picked up his cup and took another sip. His eyes fixed themselves on the video game players. Sus finished the coffee and put down the cup. "These boys are very good at the game."

Alex nodded. "They should be. They spend all their spare time and money in here."

"Are you good, Alex?"

Alex shrugged. "Not bad. Jim and I have games at home that plug into our TVs. We don't have to spend all our money in places like this."

Sus nodded. "Could I try these games here?"

Alex was somewhat taken aback. "I suppose so." He stuck his hand into his pocket and pulled out one silver coin. "Ten pence. Enough for one go."

They pushed back their chairs and walked over to the video games. One of the players, a small red headed boy, was in the final desperate phase of his ten pence worth, as he waggled the control stick and pushed buttons to ward off the endless streams of electronic UFOs attacking Earth Base. A frantic beep sounded and the video screen picture erupted into a red cloud.

MISSION FAILED...GAME OVER...flashed on the screen.

YOUR SCORE WAS 96,500. CONGRATULATIONS… PLEASE INSERT YOUR NAME ON THE CHAMPION TABLE.

The red head cursed quietly as he keyed in his name "BERT."

"Pretty good, Bert," said Alex. "Third best this week."

The boy turned. "So what?" He stuck his hands in his pockets and walked off.

Alex shrugged and turned to Sus. "They take it pretty seriously, as you can see."

Sus had moved up to the vacated game. His hands lightly touched the controls. "You have to put money in," said Alex, leaning forward and slipping the coin into the slot. The screen sprang into life. "INVASION EARTH." The letters flashed across the screen.

An electronic voice spoke up.

"WELCOME DEFENDER. EARTH IS BEING INVADED BY AN ALIEN SPACE FLEET. YOU, DEFENDER, ARE THE LAST LINE OF DEFENSE FOR BASE HEADQUARTERS. YOU ARE AT THE CONTROLS OF A DEFENCE FORCE SPACE FIGHTER X40. THE BLACK CONTROL LEVER DIRECTS YOUR FIGHTER. THE RED BUTTON ON THE LEVER FIRES THE LASER GUNS. THE YELLOW BUTTON ON THE RIGHT CONTROLS SPEED. THE BLUE BUTTON ACTIVATES YOUR DEFENCE SHIELD FOR THREE SECONDS ONLY. WHEN YOU ARE READY, PRESS THE RED BUTTON. IF YOUR FIGHTER RECEIVES TEN HITS FROM ENEMY MISSILES, IT WILL BE

DESTROYED AND THE GAME WILL BE OVER.
GOOD LUCK."

Sus waggled the control stick several times and tapped the
buttons with his other hand. He turned to Alex and smiled.
"Shall we begin?"

"Just press the red button," said Alex.

Lights swept across the steamed up the café window. A
car had passed by. Alex ran to the window and wiped an
area clear with his hand. He put his face close to the glass,
cupping his hands over his eyes to block out the café lights.
There was no sign of a car outside, only the same cluster of
parked motorbikes. He turned back. Sus was engrossed in the
video game. Mrs. Black gave him a weary look and took the
cigarette from her lip and waved it toward Sus, dropping ash
on the counter in the process. "Yer friend is a bit old for that?"

" He's been out of the country for a while. Video games
are new to him."

The woman sniffed. "He must have been far out. North
pole was it?"

Alex nodded. "Something like that. Do you have a phone
I could use?"

"What do you think this is, the North British Hotel?"

"I need to call a friend."

"Well, you can use the phone box down the street." She
turned away and started to empty a tray of dirty dishes into
a wash up sink.

There was a buzz of animated conversation behind him.
He turned quickly. Sus was still deeply engrossed in his
game. Now he was surrounded by a small group of young
onlookers who had abandoned their own games to watch.
Alex moved quickly across the room. The red headed boy,

Bert, was among them. Open mouthed, he turned to Alex. "This bloke is magic."

Alex leaned over to view the screen. 155,900...160,000... 165,000...170,000.

The score panel at the top of the screen flickered continually as Sus waggled the control and punched the buttons. UFOs disintegrated in rapid succession as they zoomed into the picture. Sus's face was expressionless, but his hands moved like a concert pianist over the controls. 200,000...250,000...300,000. A burst of spontaneous clapping broke out from the onlookers. Mrs. Black, red faced, and waving a dishcloth, had come storming from behind the counter toward the disturbance. "What's going on here? Stop all this racket. This isn't a pub you're in." She flicked her dishcloth at the heads of the onlookers as she ploughed in amongst them.

Bert held his arms up, putting himself between her and Sus. "Leave him be, Mrs. Black. He's about to set up a new record." The boy pressed home his advantage. "Your café will be famous if he breaks the world record, Mrs. Black. You will be in the newspapers and maybe TV."

Mrs. Black's expression softened slightly. She lightly patted her grey locks with her free hand. Her eyes took on a distant look, which only lasted a few seconds. "Well, keep the noise down, or I'll have to throw you all out." She turned away and beat a dignified retreat to her counter.

450,000...500,000...A burst of muted applause broke out. Alex, like the rest, had his eyes fixed on the screen. A waft of cold air blew some napkins off the tables. Mrs. Black shouted out, "This isn't a cow field. If you're coming inside shut the door?" Alex looked toward the entrance. Standing in the doorway was McCracken.

CHAPTER 12

cCRACKEN STEPPED BACKWARD INTO THE night, closing the door behind him. Alex tried to get Sus's attention, but he was still deeply engrossed in the video game. Alex moved over to the nearest window and used his fingertips to clear a small area of steamed up glass. A car was in the process of parking opposite the café. It had yellow headlights. A beeping sound filled the room, accompanied by a variety of youthful whoops. An electronic voice sounded over the bedlam.

"CONGRATULATIONS, DEFENDER, YOU HAVE DESTROYED ALL INCOMING MARTIAN ATTACKSHIPS. EARTH BASE IS SECURE. YOUR SCORE IS THE MAXIMUM 700,000. WELL DONE!"

Alex turned; Sus was surrounded by backslapping young admirers. The café doorbell tinkled as four tough looking, leather jacketed young men sauntered in. They stepped aside and Nick Stoddart strode in, his nose heavily taped in elastoplast. His eyes swept the room and came to rest on Alex and Sus. "We've been looking all over for you two. We have some unfinished business." Just then, the café doorbell jingled. McCracken entered followed another man. They walked slowly up toward the counter, apparently oblivious to the tense atmosphere.

Mrs. Black appeared from the backroom. She screwed her face into the semblance of a smile. "Mr. McCracken! What can I do for you?"

"Two coffees please, Mrs. Black." As he spoke, McCracken glanced toward Alex. He smiled, but his eyes glinted with menace. There was a sudden commotion behind Alex. He turned quickly. Stoddart and his followers had gone over to the video game area and seized hold of Sus.

Mrs. Black stomped from behind the counter. "Enough of that you lot! Out of here, or I'll get the police."

McCracken and his companion had moved to block the doorway. "I think you need to take your hands off this gentleman, young man." Stoddart stared at McCracken for a few seconds. A flicker of indecision appeared in his eyes. He turned to his cohorts for support but they all looked decidedly nervous.

Alex looked around the room in desperation. Bert, the red headed video player was close by. Alex moved next to him and whispered, "I need to get my friend away from here."

The boy screwed up his freckled face. "Old McCracken is helping him."

"I can't explain, but McCracken is going to harm my friend. I need to get him out of here, Bert."

"You want a diversion. How much is it worth?"

Alex stuck his hand in his pocket and pulled out a red, multi-blade knife and held it out to Bert. "Would this do?"

"A Swiss Army Knife! Are you kidding?"

"No, if you help me get my friend out of here, it's yours." He placed the knife in Bert's hand.

Bert looked at an inscription on the handle. "It's got your name on it."

"No...That's my brother's name."

"Tom Watts! He's the guy that got killed in the Falklands." Bert shook his head. "He's your brother, why would you want to give away his knife?"

"I wouldn't be doing it if it wasn't important."

Bert stared at him for a moment, then pushed the knife back in Alex's hand and walked away.

The standoff between Stoddart's gang and McCracken and his companion was still going on, but the village bully's resolve was beginning to wilt under the UFO investigator's gaze. Something flew over Alex's head and struck McCracken's man right between the eyes. His reaction was instantaneous. He punched Stoddart on the point of his nose. For the second time that night, blood spurted across Stoddart's face as he fell backward. With screams of anger, his four companions jumped on McCracken's man and threw him hard against the door. His head struck the frame. Glass shattered on the floor. Through the broken glass Alex saw three men running toward the doorway. They scrambled into the room, crunching through broken glass, and set about stopping Stoddart's gang. A meat pie whizzed over Alex's head and landed in the midst of the brawl at the front door. He turned quickly, just in time to see Bert ducking down behind the café counter. One of Stoddart's cronies gathered up what remained of the pie and lobbed it back toward the counter, just as Mrs.Black came hurtling out of the back room, wielding a broom. The mushy remains of the meat pie splattered across her face. Alex could see no sign of Sus. Something struck him on his forehead and dropped at his feet. It was a scone. He looked across to the counter. Mrs. Black stood behind it, red faced and screaming, her hair adorned with meat pie remnants, randomly selecting bakery items from the display shelves to launch indiscriminately into the brawling mob. Alex pushed his way through the mass of struggling bodies toward the video games area. There he found Sus, slumped in the corner. He had a bruise on his forehead.

"What a shindig, eh?" Alex whirled round. It was Bert grinning broadly. "How was that for a diversion?" He then saw Sus. "What's happened to him?"

"I think he got hit on the head," Alex looked back across the turmoil in the room. There was no sign of McCracken. He turned to the Bert. "Can you help me get him out of here?"

Bert nodded, "Okay, but let's do it quick. The police will be here any minute. I need to go." He bent down and took hold of one of Sus's arms. Alex took the other. They hauled Sus to his feet and began working their way around the wall toward the door, using the video machines as cover. Some of McCracken's men were still locked in a struggle with the Stoddart's gang members. There was still no sign of McCracken, but two more of his men blocked the entrance.

"We'll never get out that way," said Bert. "Let's try the store room at the back of the shop. It has a door that takes you out to the back street. They hustled Sus along the wall to the rear. He had regained some of his strength and was able to support himself.

Alex stumbled over something, almost losing his balance. It was the outstretched figure of McCracken, surrounded by broken pottery. Mrs. Black was kneeling beside him, lifting his head and mumbling to herself in the process. "Oh dear, dear!" She turned a chastened face to Alex. "I took a swing at one of those roughnecks with my teapot and it slipped out of my hand and hit poor Mr. McCracken, right on the back of his head."

Alex and Bert steered Sus behind the counter. Alex kicked open the store-room door and they bundled Sus inside. Bert slammed the door shut behind them. A single, dusty and grease-covered light bulb, hanging at the end of a frayed cord, provided some dim illumination. On every wall were shelves packed with tins and other supplies for the café.

They dragged Sus toward the back door. Alex stretched out his hand and grabbed the doorknob. It turned easily. He pulled the door open a crack and listened. There was no sound. Cautiously, he peeked out into the dark street. It seemed deserted. There was a sound from behind. The door back into to the café started to open slowly, a gloved hand appeared. Alex threw his weight against the door. A muffled scream came from the other side as the door slammed shut. The finger-tips of the leather glove remained in view, caught between the door and the jamb. Alex slid the rusty bolt lock closed. Sounds of frantic activity came from the café. Alex looked around for some weapon but all that was in the room was the stock on the shelves. He grabbed two tins of condensed milk and waited for the enemy's next move. The glove disappeared as somebody tugged it free from the other side.

They sat Sus down on the floor, leaning his back against the wall.

Bert looked at Alex. "There is something really weird about all of this. Who is he? Why are those men out to get him?"

The distant sound of a police siren carried on the cold draft of air that drifted into the storeroom. There were sounds of increased activity from the café. Alex turned toward the door, weighing the condensed milk tins in each hand. Bert moved toward the back door. "I'm sorry. I need to go. If I get nabbed by the police my mum will have my guts for garters."

Alex nodded. "Thanks for your help, Bert. You did great. I can take it from here."

Bert nodded. "No problem." He pulled the door open and charged out into the night.

Alex listened till the clatter of Bert's footsteps faded away. He threw down the cans and hauled Sus to his feet. Sus still seemed dazed, but was able to stand. Alex hesitated for a moment at the opening and hitched his arm around Sus. He took a deep breath, shivering as the cold air struck his flushed face. He took a firm hold on Sus's arm and stepped out the door. Distant sounds of angry shouting filled the night air, but Alex stared straight ahead as he and Sus stumbled over the slippery cobbles like entrants in a drunken three-legged race, their gasping breath trailing behind them. Headlights appeared at the end of the street. Alex tried to swerve to one side. His feet slipped on the cobbles. He and Sus tumbled to the ground as the car screeched to a halt alongside.

CHAPTER 13

C AR DOORS CREAKED OPEN AND feet clattered on the cobbles. Two figures were silhouetted against the headlights. Alex scrambled to his feet, fists clenched. Somebody grabbed his arm.

"Take it easy, pal." It was Jim. He turned toward to the other person. Even in the dark the white clerical collar stood out.

"Mr. Dickson? How did you guys get here?"

The minister was already helping Sus to his feet. "Divine intervention, I think. We were taking a short cut to your house. We will fill in the rest later. Let's remove ourselves from this area as soon as possible."

Twenty minutes later Alex, Jim, Sus, and Mr. Dickson were sitting in the study at the manse, along with Fiona and her mother. Shelves of books lined the walls and the odor of their ancient leather bindings permeated the room. Mrs. Dickson had distributed cups of tea and a plate of shortbread. Sus looked pale and drawn, but had regained some of his strength. His eyes took in every detail of the room as he sipped the hot beverage.

Mr. Dickson, sitting at his desk, put down his cup. "I

think the best way to start is for me to explain what I have experienced tonight." He leaned forward on his elbows and clasped his hands under his chin. "At church service tonight, after the police had left with Mr. Sus, an unusual thing happened to me. As we began to sing a hymn, I put on my reading glasses and found my vision was blurred. At first I thought that I had picked up somebody else's glasses. I took them off to look. They were my glasses, no doubt about that. Then I realized that I could see the words clearly—without my glasses." Mr. Dickson continued, "That wasn't the end of it. Mr. Tait came up to me after the service to inform me how he disliked the way I had shouted during my sermon."

"But he's deaf," said Fiona. "He's always complaining that you don't speak loud enough."

Mr. Dickson nodded. "Very true, Fiona, so I asked him to check out his hearing-aid." The minister smiled. "It was working fine. That was the problem. He could hear quite normally without it."

Alex glanced at Sus. He had been paying close attention to the minister's words. Mr. Dickson stood up and began to walk back and forth across the floor. "Rose and I had only been back in the manse a short while when we had visitors, Mr. and Mrs. Adams. They were handing in a box of food for our church food pantry to distribute to the needy families of striking miners. They were doing this in gratitude for the sudden improvement in Mr. Adams's health and well-being. He had lost his desire for alcohol."

Rose Dickson shook her head. "It's really amazing. He already looks ten years younger."

"What's happening, Dad?"

"What has happened, Fiona, is that in the space of one evening, several individuals in this village have been healed of a variety of ailments. First, there was your blood condition, then my eyesight, Mr. Tait's hearing, and Mr. Adams's alcoholism." He stopped pacing and turned toward Sus. "I thought hard about the connection between all these events. I believe God still does give miraculous answers to prayer but, apart from Fiona's case, I am not aware there had been much in the way of any intercession for the others." He looked at Sus. "However, all these people had one thing in common. They had recently come into physical contact with our friend, Mr. Sus."

He paused for a moment. "Then I got a phone call from Sergeant Brown's wife. I had called her earlier to find out how Bill was doing. At that time she was still waiting to hear from her husband. He had gone with Bill in the ambulance to the Royal Infirmary. Bill's head injury was really bad. The ambulance crew had told Sergeant Brown that it was the worst they had ever seen. We prayed together and I asked her to give me a call when she had any news."

"Did she call?"

"She did indeed Fiona. She was, to say the least, very excited. She said our prayer had been answered. Bill was going to be fine. There was no indication of brain damage. He was fully conscious and able to talk. The doctors said it was a miracle." He paused, "It was only when I hung up the phone that the penny dropped. I now understood what all these healed people had in common." He looked at Sus; "They had all come into physical contact with you my friend."

"How can you possibly know that Dad?"

"I did some research Fiona. Mr.Tait was one of those helping me to eject Sus from the church service. I spoke to Frank, the constable who was on duty with Bill. When Mr. Adams was picked up, Sus was in the car with him. When Bill was injured at the pit they tried to lay him on the back seat of the police car. Sus was already there." He turned to Alex, "You witnessed that."

Alex nodded. " Sergeant Brown dragged Sus out, dumped him on the road and drove off." Alex put his hand in his pocket to get his handkerchief. His fingers closed around his inhaler. He pulled it out and stared at for some seconds.

"What's wrong, Alex?" asked Fiona.

"It's my inhaler. The last time I needed to use it was when Jim and I were climbing up Jake's Law."

All eyes were now fixed on Sus. He looked from one to another. He rose slowly to his feet and walked over to the window. The curtains had not been drawn. A slight snowfall had started and the light spilling out of the room illuminated the white flakes drifting down into the back garden. He turned and looked at Alex. "I now understand my growing weakness," he said softly.

"It is not just when you get too far from Jake's Law?" said Alex.

"No Alex, that is only part of the problem."

"What problem?" Mr. Dickson's tone was tinged with some exasperation. "After speaking to Mrs. Brown, I went to the Hood's house. Jim told me all about your arrival and the other events. I now believe you are not of this world, Sus. Why have you come?"

Alex turned to Sus. "Tell them what you told me up on the Law."

Sus was silent for a moment. "My mission was to give this information to the leaders of your world. We were concerned that, should the general population know what was about to occur, panic would set in. Your people are just beginning exploration of the cosmos and we would prefer your contact with our civilization to develop more gradually. However, now I have little choice but to share it with you." Sus proceeded to retell the story of the outer galactic civil war, Tan's plan to invade Earth, Sus's desperate mission to warn the Earth of the danger, and the chilling understanding that agents of Tan were already operating in the country. When he finished, a stunned silence settled over the room.

A shaken, pale faced Mr. Dickson was the first to speak up. "Is there anything that we can do?"

Sus shook his head. "Not at the present stage of technical progress on Earth. That is why my father has sent me."

Jim was puzzled. "Why couldn't your father send a fleet to destroy Tan's fleet?"

"Tan will arrive in this area of the galaxy long before our fastest manned space cruisers could overtake his invasion fleet."

"But how did you get here before him Sus?" asked Fiona.

"The vehicle I arrived in is an untested experimental prototype, only one of which exists, capable of transporting only one passenger. To allow my body to withstand the journey, its molecular structure was altered for the duration of the flight and then reestablished when I landed."

Jim spoke up. "Was that the gas cloud?"

Sus nodded. "My body was reestablished in a form that would conform to the inhabitants of this world. The gas cloud was part of the process of rehabilitation. My molecules have been reformed in a body, which is a composite of Alex, Jim, and others within the area who were touched by the cloud's tracer beams. I have the characteristics of them all."

"That's how you knew how to head-butt?" said Jim.

Sus nodded. "I'm afraid so, Jim. I have taken on some of

the instincts and attributes of those the beams touched, good and otherwise."

Jim grinned. "Your light probes must have contacted somebody coming out of the pub."

"What exactly is this beacon on top of Jake's Law, Sus?" asked Mr. Dickson.

"A navigational landing device that is buried deep into the core of the hill. It allowed my craft to transfer from the Earth's orbit into a spiral descent to the surface."

Rose Dickson spoke up for the first time. "But why choose to land here, Sus?"

Sus shrugged his shoulders. "Why indeed? I was supposed to land near to your nation's capital, London, your center of national government, but something was wrong. There are many such beacon stations scattered over this country, but the only one still operating is here on Jake's Law. I have also discovered that the stability and structure of my body depends on my staying close to the beacon. As Alex and I found out, I cannot go much further than the outskirts of the village."

"But if you cannot get to our leaders, we must get them to come to you."

Sus smiled grimly. "That will have to be very soon, Mr. Dickson."

"Is Tan's fleet as close as that?"

Sus shook his head. "They will not arrive here for some time." He glanced toward Alex. "I thought the state of my weakness solely depended on my proximity to the beacon on Jake's Law. Now, after listening to you, Mr. Dickson, I understand I have another problem."

"What is that?" asked Mr. Dickson.

"My people have, over the centuries, developed very

powerful defense systems in their blood, which aggressively attack and destroy all disease. There is little or no sickness on my world, but here on Earth..."

Mr. Dickson frowned. "But how does that explain the people here who have been healed by coming into contact with you?"

"The process which restructured my body has been less than perfect. It would seem that when I come into contact with your people, my body absorbs any sickness they have. This accelerates the dissipation of my body structure. By staying close to the beacon I can slow down the process, but the composition of my body will continue to weaken. My only hope is to return to my world, but that is now impossible."

"Why can't you leave the way you came?" asked Mr. Dickson.

"The craft I arrived in is now on a far out orbit around Earth. To summon it back, I need to trigger off the beacon on top off the hill."

"The column of blue light we saw?" said Jim.

"Yes," said Sus. "That was activated by a signal from my craft as we orbited Earth. To bring the craft back I need to activate the beam from the hilltop." He turned to Mr. Dickson. "The trigstone that would allow me to do this has been removed from the hilltop."

"What is it?" asked Mr. Dickson.

"Sus showed me the hole the trigstone goes into," said Alex. "It's not very big. Maybe a foot deep, cylindrical in shape. It's in the flat rock outcrop that forms the floor of the wee chapel."

"The device looks like a stone?" said Mr. Dickson.

"It will have the color and texture of rock," said Sus, "But it has a trigger device built into it."

"It would be a long shot, but we can ask some of the older folks in the village and maybe find who removed it," said the minister.

Sus shook his head. "I'm afraid the trigstone was removed a long, long time ago."

"How long?" asked Mr. Dickson.

"About five hundred of your years," said Sus.

The minister's mouth fell open in astonishment. "That would be in the fourteen hundreds?"

"If you cannot leave, what will happen, Sus?" Fiona asked.

"Before your sun rises tomorrow, I shall be dead."

A blanket of silence fell over the room broken only by the steady ticking of the wall clock.

Sus held up his hands. "My friends, I still have a mission to complete. That is why I came. Your world is about to be invaded by the forces of Tan. He has already placed some of his people here who have been making preparations for the invasion. Some of them may have been here for years, promoting social unrest, anarchy, and chaos." He turned to Mr. Dickson. "When did McCracken first appear in the village?"

The minister thought for a moment. "It must be about three years ago...yes, that would be right. He bought Deil's Quarry Cottage and the land, including the quarry itself."

Rose Dickson spoke up. "He has never worked the quarry as a business though, has he Stuart?"

Mr. Dickson nodded. "That's true, but then, no one else did before him, at least since before World War I."

"Why was that?" said Sus.

"Well, as you can tell by its name, Deil's Quarry had something of a curse on it. Deil is an old Scot's word for devil. Ever since it's beginnings, last century there were reports of strange sicknesses that affected the workers. Country folk have always been a superstitious lot, and still are, even in these enlightened times."

"Mr. McCracken also moved here around the same time as we had all that business about the crop circles," said Mrs. Dickson.

Sus raised his eyebrows. "Crop circles?"

Mr. Dickson nodded. "Yes, actually there were several reports from all over the country. Crops, especially in wheat fields, flattened down to form strange shapes, mostly circular. Then, one appeared in farmer Wallace's wheat field and we had all sorts of experts and eccentrics visiting the area."

"What was their explanation for the circles?"

Mr. Dickson shrugged. "They came up with a wide variety of theories...whirlwinds, magnetic forces, druids, UFOs and hoaxers. You name it."

"That was when McCracken arrived?" Sus asked quietly.

Mr. Dickson nodded. "Yes...he was one of the more eccentric. He claimed it was all a government plot to disguise the fact they had discovered an alternative power source. The press and TV people played him for all he was worth for a few days."

"What happened then?" asked Sus.

Mr. Dickson sighed. "I'm afraid it got pretty crazy. More circles appeared in fields all around the village, some were obvious hoaxes and the subject became something of a joke and the media lost interest."

Sus nodded his head. "Tan has obviously been landing scouting teams here for some years. They would not be able to use the beacon that brought me. They would use cloaking devices, which would allow them to land with little chance of being observed. However the crop circles may well have occurred at sites where Tan's advance scouting ships initially landed. Some circles may have been simple hoaxes, but McCracken could well have been behind some of these fake circles to divert any serious investigation. I suspect the purchase of the quarry provided a secluded landing area, hidden from the village by Jake's Law. However, as with my landing, there would be some risk of being spotted by one of your people. If someone in your village did see a real landing incident, who would they go to? Their friends and the police would think they were crazy. But Mr. McCracken, the UFO Investigator, would believe them. He would be the one they could risk telling about what they had seen."

"What would he do?" asked Mr. Dickson.

"He would silence them."

Alex felt the hair rise on the back of his neck. He stuck his hand into his pocket and took out the bronze medallion. "You better look at this, Mr. Dickson."

The minister picked up the medallion from Alex's open palm. He turned it over. "A. Blyth? Andy Blyth? Where did you find it Alex?"

"In Mr. McCracken's cottage."

The minister's face went white. "What can we do, Sus?"

Sus placed his hand on Mr. Dickson's shoulder. "The odds are not all in Tan's favor. His fleet is powerful, but not large. He would like to take over this planet with as little opposition as possible. Tan need recruits for his plans as well as infrastructure. He does not want to destroy Earth. He wants to enslave it. If I could reach your leaders, I could provide a defense that could defeat Tan's evil purpose, or at least delay him till my father's forces catch up with him. But if Tan can establish a base here, then the whole galaxy is at risk. The problem is, I cannot leave this village." He looked at them all in turn, "My friends, we have to find some way to get my message to your leaders." He suddenly looked very weary. "My time is limited."

Mr. Dickson leaned back on his desktop and massaged the back of his neck with his hand. "The only people who might take an interest would be the newspapers...or the TV." He raised his eyebrows a fraction. "The BBC TV crew who came out to cover the trouble at the pit are staying overnight at the Justinlees Inn. They are expecting more action from the pickets tomorrow morning." He turned to Sus. "I will tell them it will be the biggest scoop in the history of television. That should whet their appetite."

Sus looked troubled. "My message is only meant for your leaders. It is not for all your people."

Mr. Dickson shook his head. "I totally understand, my friend, but this is the only way you will get their attention. If you can convince them your story is for real, they will be able to pass it on to the proper authorities." Mr. Dickson jumped up. "I will drive up to the inn and talk to the BBC chaps. He turned to Alex. "I think it would be safer if you and Sus wait in the church."

Turning to Jim, "You can stay with Rose and Fiona here in the manse, Jim."

A few minutes later, Mr. Dickson, Alex, and Sus were crunching across the gravel to the rear of the church. Alex shivered after the warmth of the minister's study. He looked toward the dark mass of trees that surrounded the church. McCracken and his accomplices were out there somewhere. He shivered once more, but this time, not because of the chill air.

CHAPTER 14

THE MINISTER OPENED THE VESTRY door and ushered them inside. He walked over to the small open fire and jabbed at the coals with the poker. A flicker of flame sprang up. "I thought it was warmer in here than usual." He replaced the poker on the hook beside the fireplace. "Mr. Pryde, our beadle, must have been back to the church tonight. Trying to solve our condensation problem, I suppose." He straightened up. "If and when the TV crew gets here, I will bring them over here to the church."

Alex nodded his head. Sus seemed more interested in the pictures of past ministers that covered the walls. "Is this a very old building?" said Sus.

The minister nodded. "Very much so. Built in 1727." He smiled. "Mind you, this is the second church building in this area. The first was really St. Jacob's Chapel. It was several centuries older than this place. The site was pretty close to here. Just on the other side of the Monkland Wall that the monks built back in the twelfth century. It marks the old abbey's boundary." He glanced at his wristwatch. "I must be on my way." He strode to the door and pulled it open. "If you want to know anything about the history of this place, have a word with Archie." He winked. "Make sure you get him to tell you about the ghost." The door closed and the sound of his feet crunching through the snow faded into the distance.

Alex glanced at Sus. The alien looked pale and thoughtful as he stared at the flickering flames in the fireplace. "We might as well have a seat." Alex pulled an old oak chair from behind a small table and placed it before the fire. Sus sat down. Alex dragged another chair over beside him. He held out his chilled hands to the flames.

A sound came from behind the sanctuary door. The brass doorknob began to slowly turn. The hair on Alex's neck stood up. The door itself opened an inch or so then stopped. A wisp of blue smoke curled through the narrow opening into the vestry.

"Is that you, Minister?" The voice was low and husky.

Alex sighed with relief and jumped to his feet. "Come in, Mr. Pryde, it's alright." The door swung quickly open and a small gray haired elderly man edged his way into the vestry. He looked from Alex to Sus then back to Alex. The expression on his face was a mixture of relief and annoyance. He was clad in a dark suit, shiny with age. One hand was behind his back and a thin column of blue smoke rose up above him.

"It's you, young Watts." He straightened up and glanced at the fireplace. "Och, the fire's almost out. I better nip out and get a drop more coal." He began to edge toward the outside door. "I'll just be a minute." He flashed a brief smile and opening the door slipped out. The door slammed shut behind him.

Alex turned to Sus and smiled. "Jim's mum says Archie is the only person in the village who doesn't know that everybody knows he smokes."

Sus looked puzzled. "He is always burning?"

Alex grinned. "No. He isn't burning—the smoke was from a cigarette he was hiding behind his back."

Sus looked even more puzzled. "Cigarette? What is cigarette?"

Alex searched his mind for a simple explanation. "It's a paper tube with ground up leaves inside. You light the end and stick it in your mouth."

"Does that not cause pain?" said Sus.

Alex giggled, "No! You don't put the burning end in your mouth. That stays outside. You suck in the smoke. It's a drug. It seems to help people relax. The doctors say it is bad for your health."

The beadle reappeared, loaded down with a bucket full of coal. "Now, we'll get this fire going again. It's a raw night outside." He tipped coal, straight from the bucket, into the fire. "She'll be going great guns in no time." He put down the bucket and adjusted the damper. He suddenly went into a spasm of violent coughing. He leaned on the mantelpiece until the coughing had stopped. He took out a large handkerchief and brushed it across his mouth. He looked at the handkerchief then stuck it hastily into his pocket.

"Are you alright, Mr. Pryde?" Alex asked.

"Och, aye, lad. Too many years at the pit face, breathing in stone dust, plays up a wee bit with my lungs now and again but I am fine." He turned to face Sus. "I havena met this gentleman. Here to see the minister, I suppose?" He held out his hand. "Archie Pryde...I'm the church beadle." He straightened his back as he spoke.

The alien rose to his feet and took hold of the hand. "My name is Sus and I am a friend, Archie Pryde."

The old man raised his eyebrows a fraction and cast a quizzical look at Alex.

"Sus is a visitor to this country," Alex said quickly.

"Oh aye, that is very nice." The old man's voice was less than enthusiastic. "From Europe, I suppose?"

"No....not Europe exactly," Alex's words fell over each other. The old man looked more confused than ever and another question started to form on his lips. Alex cut in before the words could form. "He is very interested in the history of the church. Mr. Dickson said you were the best person to talk to about that."

A look of quiet satisfaction drifted across the beadle's face. "Well, I suppose I have picked up a good few tales about this place in the thirty years I have been the beadle." He rubbed his hands together. "Of course, I was telt a lot by my old father. He was the beadle before me, you ken? It's been a family tradition." He turned to Sus. "Let me show you around the sanctuary, Mr. Sus. There are some very interesting things in there." Wasting no time, the old man pulled open the door and stepped into the sanctuary, followed by Alex and Sus. The church lights were set very dim. The illumination from the street lamps, diffused through the stained glass of the giant arched windows, cast eerie patches of color across the pews.

Mr. Pryde began by pointing out the names of each of the apostles that were commemorated on eleven of the windows. Sus did not speak until they stood before the twelfth window. The figure was not upright like the others. Instead, he lay on his side with his head pillowed on a green rock. In the background was a hill from the top of which a crystal blue spiral stairway stretched up into a golden sky, with angels ascending and descending.

"What is this?" Sus asked.

"Och, that is 'Jacob's Ladder.' It is a story in the Bible."

"Has this window anything to do with the St. Jacob's Chapel?" asked Alex.

Mr. Pryde shrugged. "I suppose it does, lad."

"What happened to the chapel?" asked Alex.

"About the time of the Reformation, the abbey was taken away from the monks and the chapel was destroyed by witch hunters. They said the building was haunted. Strange noises and lights had been reported coming from the chapel in the dead of night. They set fire to the chapel and it burned to the ground."

Alex turned to Mr. Pryde. "Were all these stained glass windows put in when this church was built?"

The beadle shook his head. "No, they started to run out of money before the church was finished. The Marquis of Newbattle pitched in money to help out. They were so grateful they asked him if there was any part of the new building they could dedicate to him. He asked them to put in the Jacob's Ladder window. They were not all that keen, mind you."

"Why not?" said Alex.

"Well, they were a very severe and sober bunch, and did not believe in decoration which would take away from the worship of God." He smiled. "Of course, they couldna very well refuse; they needed the marquis' gold." He waved his hand toward the other windows. "As the years passed, the church folk became a bit less strict and they put in more stained glass."

"Why did the marquis choose the Jacob's Ladder picture?" asked Alex.

The old man shrugged. "Nobody seems to know for sure. It was one of the marquis' ancestors who was given the abbey property after the monks got chased out during the Reformation. The king made him the first Marquis of

Newbattle. In 1727, when the marquis at that time helped with the building of the new church, he handed over some items from the chapel that the monks had managed to save when the mob set the building on fire. One of the monks died in the fire."

"What were the items?" asked Alex.

"Och, a bunch of old hand written books the monks had put together. Must have taken them years to do one book."

"What were the books about?" said Alex.

The old man smiled. "Dinna ask me, laddie. They are all in Latin. They have some bonnie pictures though. They're in the minister's study, in the bookcase with the glass doors. The museum in Edinburgh tried to get a hold of them several times in the past, but the Kirk folk wouldna part with them." The old man's face took on a thoughtful look and he stroked his chin with gnarled fingers. "It has been a long time since I looked at them, but I remember my old father showing me a picture in one that was just like the stained glass window."

"Jacob's Ladder?" said Alex

"Aye, Jacob's Ladder." Mr. Pryde pointed toward the front of the sanctuary. "The old baptismal font over there came from the chapel. Every bairn in the church since 1727 has been baptized out of it."

They all went over to have a closer look. The font was made of dark granite and stood about four feet high. It was a simple design. The bowl was carved out of an octagonal shaped block of stone. It was supported by an octagonal stone pillar resting on a square slab base. Mr. Pryde leaned over to look in the bowl. "Well, there's a queer thing."

"What's wrong?" asked Alex.

The old man scratched the side of his head. "There is no water left in the bowl. We just had a baptism a few days ago and it was threequarters full. I will fill it tonight before I leave. There is a baptism next Sunday."

"Mr. Dickson said something about a ghost," said Alex.

"He means the Grey Monk." Mr. Pryde shook his head. "The minister thinks it's a bit of a joke."

Alex struggled to stifle a smile. "Have you seen it, Mr. Pryde?"

The old man shook his head slowly. "No, I havna, lad, but my old father did. He was beadle during the war and one night, he saw the Grey Monk." He shook his head once more. "He wasnae the first to see it either. The church records mention folk seeing it several times in the past two hundred years."

"Who was the Grey Monk?" asked Alex.

The beadle sighed. "He was the monk who died trying to save the books and things from the burning chapel. Then, when the new church was built, his ghost began to appear."

The vestry door burst open and Fiona shot into the sanctuary. "Mr. Pryde, Mum needs your help. She's having trouble with the furnace."

The beadle left the sanctuary in some haste.

Fiona walked down the aisle. "Has Archie been telling you the old wife's tale about the Grey Monk?"

Alex nodded. "He did that."

A creaking sound echoed through the building.

"Somebody's opening the front door," whispered Fiona.

Alex felt the hair rise on the back of his neck. To the right of the pulpit was a small arched door, which was the entrance into the sanctuary from the vestibule at the base of the bell tower. Newbattle Church was unusual in that the main access to the sanctuary was from the front, through double doors in the wall of the bell tower. Alex noticed someone move up alongside him. It was Sus, his eyes fixed on the door. He seemed tense.

The small door swung open. A cold draft touched Alex's face and a flurry of fine snow wafted through the opening. A dark figure was framed in the arched doorway. It stood still for a moment, then, stepped into the sanctuary. Alex drew a sharp breath. He had seen the sharp angular face, with its neatly trimmed black moustache before on the television news. It was Mr. Steel, the union leader.

"Das?...Is it you, Das?" Sus said quietly.

CHAPTER 15

WHITE TEETH SHOWED UP ON the dark shadow of the visitor's face. "Yes, Lord Sus, it is I, your loyal servant, Das." He stepped forward into the dim light of the sanctuary, closing the door behind him. "The humble body form you have assumed is remarkable, Lord Sus. You should have been more selective in your choice of donors."

"How long have you been here, Das?" said Sus.

"Almost two earth years, Lord Sus. Emperor Tan has had advance teams here for much longer."

Sus nodded his head slowly. "When you did not return from the battle zone, we thought you had died."

"I almost did, Lord Sus. Emperor Tan took me prisoner. He spared my life."

"Now you serve him?"

Das shrugged. "I support him. I believe he has the vision that your father lacks. The Federation has become feeble and without direction. It has not grown since your father became President. It must expand or die."

"My father brought peace, the first for many generations." There was an edge to Sus's voice that Alex had not heard before. "Your master, Tan, was not satisfied with being one of the leading members of the Council. He wanted complete power, even if that led to the destruction of the Alliance."

"Better to risk destruction than maintain mediocrity, my Lord Sus."

Sus raised his right arm and pointed a finger at Das. "He failed on both accounts. Tan has been defeated. The revolt has collapsed."

Das shook his head. "You are mistaken, Lord Sus. Emperor Tan lost a battle, not the war. He will establish a new capital here on Earth and expand his control in this sector of the galaxy. He will launch another assault against the Alliance and this time will not fail."

Sus shook his head slowly. "His army has been decimated. It is over, Das."

Just then a police siren sounded outside the church and a chorus of muffled shouts and the dull clatter of running feet followed. Das sneered. "Listen, Lord Sus. Hear the future servants of Tan: the new army of revolution."

"This world is very young, Das. They are centuries behind us in technology and science. They will not suit your purposes."

Das shook his head. "I must disagree Lord Sus. The people of this planet have strength and resolve in their blood, as it was in our people before your father's policy of peace at any price, diluted it. He pointed a gloved hand at Alex and Fiona. "These and their kind will be the warriors that shall spread the Empire of Tan to the limits of the galaxy. They have untapped reservoirs of aggression that can be channeled into the service of Tan."

"I assume your time here on Earth has been spent encouraging this aggressive spirit?" said Sus.

Das smiled. "Civil unrest before invasion can be helpful."

He walked over to the pulpit and began to slowly climb the carpeted steps. "We have been able to infiltrate many important areas of society in this country." He stepped into the pulpit, resting both hands on the rail, leaning down toward them. "You have arrived much too late, Lord Sus. Much too late."

"Then why have you tried to destroy me?"

Das shrugged. "We overreacted at first. That was a misjudgment of the situation by our people here. It has exposed our existence to a few members of the native population for the first time. However, that knowledge has been restricted to this rather insignificant small group you are aligned with. They pose little threat to our operation."

"Then why are you here?"

Das raised his eyes to the ceiling, then fixed them once more on Sus. "We understand your condition, Lord Sus. You are slowly dying. You must know that? You cannot leave this village. Even to last out your remaining few hours, you must stay close to the beacon."

Fiona took hold of Alex's arm. Her fingers dug into his flesh. Das continued. "Your craft is now in a wide orbit awaiting your signal to return to pick you up. You know that will not happen, Lord Sus. You already have found out, as we have, that the trigstone is missing." He pointed at Alex and Fiona. "Their ancestors must have removed it centuries ago." He turned back to Sus. "There is no way to trigger the beacon beam to bring your craft down." He stepped out of the pulpit and started down the steps. "However, there is a solution to your problem, Lord Sus."

"What would that be, Das?" Sus asked quietly.

Das stepped off the last step and stood face to face with Sus. "You can live, Lord Sus. At first we lost some of our people but we have developed ways to deal with the weakness that is destroying you. The process by which you have drawn sickness out from others into your own body can be reversed under special conditions."

"Reversed?"

"Exactly, Lord Sus. We can obtain a healthy specimen of the human species and transfer all sickness into it."

"This healthy specimen would then die?"

Das shrugged. "It is a question of priority, Lord Sus."

"Why do you now want me alive when you have tried so hard to destroy me?"

"You present no danger to our plans, Lord Sus. You have the support of a small group of children and a few adults. Even if the whole village would support you, it would make no difference to the outcome. There is no one of influence here. None who have any access to the leaders of this nation. Earth will soon be under the total control of Tan." He strolled a few yards down the aisle, then turned. "Lord Sus, you are a member an elite ruling dynasty. In spite of the failings of your father's presidency, Tan holds your family in high esteem, as do the population masses back on Ven. He regards the termination of your existence in this situation as waste."

Sus gave a weary smile, "What does he suggest as an alternative?"

Das stepped closer to Sus, holding out his hands in a gesture of appeal. "He offers you the position of Ruler of Earth and a seat next to him on the council of the New Federation." Das lowered his hands and stepped closer. "Is the choice so difficult, Lord Sus? A life of power and influence, or a few brief hours of increasing pain and then oblivion?"

"You paint a generous picture, Das. It betrays your desperation. The power of your master, Tan, is in decline.

My father, and the forces of the Federation, will eventually overtake and eliminate the last vestiges of the rebellion. My mission was to protect the innocent people of this planet from the destructive effects of Tan's final death throes."

A shadow swept across the face of Das. Hard lines formed and the eyes glinted with malice. "You are a fool to sacrifice your life for this mediocre species."

Sus shook his head. "They have qualities of goodness and courage. In time they will become, by free choice, members of the Greater Federation."

Das snorted. "Time has run out for them, and for you, Lord Sus." He brushed past Sus and strode toward the door. He grasped the handle and pulled it open. A fresh flurry of snow blew in on an icy draft. He turned back, "If you posed any real threat to us, you would already be dead, Lord Sus. As your demise draws closer our offer may seem more acceptable." He stepped out. The door crashed closed, the sound echoing around the stone walls of the sanctuary.

CHAPTER 16

LEX EXHALED THE BREATH HE had been holding. He turned to Fiona. Her face was pale and he lower lip trembled slightly. At the rear of the sanctuary the vestry door opened.

It was Mr. Dickson. "The TV news crew is on the way." There was a screech of brakes outside. "They are here. Are you ready, Sus?"

Sus started slowly up the aisle followed by Fiona and Alex. As they entered the vestry, a young man wearing a leather jacket and carrying a clipboard stepped through the outside door. Behind him was a younger man with a TV camera perched like a parrot on his shoulder. The first man smiled at Sus. "I'm Rick James, BBC Scotland. Mr. Dickson here assures us you have something important to tell us." He nodded to the cameraman. "Okay Fred, lets take it." He brushed his hair back with his free hand as Fred handed him the microphone. He steadied himself and faced the camera.

"Good evening viewers. This is BBC Scotland, Eye Witness News, Rick James reporting. We are in the vestry of Newbattle Church in the strike torn village of Newbattle. With us we have the Reverend Stuart Dickson, the minister, and his friend...Mr. Sus, who has a message for you which the Reverend Dickson believes could well be the most important you will ever receive." He held out the microphone. "You're on, Mr. Sus."

Sus straightened up and faced the camera. "My name is Sus. I come from Planet Ven, which is located on the far side of the galaxy. I bring a warning that your planet is danger of invasion...."

The reporter threw up his arms. " Okay! That's enough..." he turned to the cameraman, "Cut it, Fred...."

Mr. Dickson stepped forward. "Mr. James...please..."

The reporter snorted. "What do you expect? You drag us down here to meet some guy dressed in an old army overcoat who is warning us about an invasion from outer space. Who do you think I am, Orson Welles?"

Alex looked toward Sus, The alien had stuck his hand inside the overcoat. "My friend," Sus's voice seemed stronger. He extended his clenched fist. "I have something here meant for your leaders...but that will not be possible." His hand opened up. Lying in the hollow of his palm was a small, pearl colored sphere.

Rick James gave a loud sigh. "Terrific..." He turned to the cameraman. "Okay, Fred, let's bag it." A pulsing sound began to fill the room. It rapidly increased in pitch and sound now seemed to be vibrating inside his head. The small sphere had begun to glow. Sus slowly lowered his hand and the sphere remained floating free in midair. The sound increased to a higher pitch. Fred the camera man was desperately focusing on the strange object. The sphere began to move in a circular path, in a vertical plane, slowly at first, but with increasing speed. The diameter of the circle it traced expanded with each rotation of the sphere. The sphere was now just a blur.

A bright spot of light appeared at the center of the circle and spread outward to fill the circle. The sound stopped. Colors swirled around in the circle. A voice filled the room, soft, but full of authority.

"PEOPLE OF EARTH, I GREET YOU IN THE NAME OF THE OUTER GALACTIC ALLIANCE. I AM PRESIDENT VAH, ELECTED LEADER OF THE ALLIANCE COUNCIL. WE WISH YOU WELL. THE ALLIANCE IS A GROUP OF PLANETS ON THE RIM OF THE GALAXY."

The face vanished and the circle went black. Points of light appeared. The picture zoomed in on one particular light. Soon it filled the screen. Green and brown shapes materialized. At first Alex thought it was Earth, just like the picture the American astronauts had taken from the moon. As the shapes became clearer he could see the land masses were different. There was no sea.

"THIS IS VEN, THE COUNCIL PLANET AND ITS CAPITAL CITY, NEWJER." A city appeared on the circle that brought further gasps of wonder from the onlookers. It was like nothing Alex had ever seen, real or imaginary. Towers of transparent material pierced the sky. Large green parks nestled between the buildings. Crystal blue rivers flowed through them. Silver spheres flitted to and fro between the buildings.

The city vanished. The shimmering face of President Vah reappeared.

"I SHOW YOU THESE PICTURES, SO YOU WILL BELIEVE THIS MESSAGE I SEND YOU. YOUR

WORLD IS IN DANGER OF BEING INVADED BY THE REBEL FORCES OF EMPEROR TAN."

Another picture appeared in the circle. Once again the star pierced blackness of space. This time there were also thirteen diamond shaped objects, all the same dull red metallic color, moving in a steady, menacing way. Alex did not need to be told what they were.

"THESE ARE THE WARSHIPS OF TAN. THEY ARE NOW CLOSE TO YOUR PART OF THE GALAXY. THE LARGEST CRAFT IS EMPEROR TAN'S FLAGSHIP. ITS TECHNOLOGY AND FIREPOWER ALONE WOULD BE SUFFICIENT TO DESTROY YOUR PLANET. THE PRESERVATION OF YOUR CIVILIZATION DEPENDS ON THE COMPLETE DESTRUCTION OF TAN AND HIS FLEET. THE ONLY SPACE CRAFT WE HAVE THAT ARE CAPABLE OF OVERTAKING TAN BEFORE HE REACHES EARTH ARE UNMANNED ROBOT SPACEFIGHTERS. FIVE ARE ALREADY CLOSING UPON TAN'S FLEET. HOWEVER THEY ARE NOW WELL BEYOND THE RANGE OF OUR CONTROL. FOR THIS REASON I HAVE SENT MY ONLY SON, SUS, TO WARN YOUR LEADERS AND PROVIDE THE TECHNOLOGY THAT WILL ENABLE THEM TO CONTROL THE SPACEFIGHTERS TO DEFEND YOUR PLANET. IF YOU ARE LISTENING TO ME NOW, IT MEANS THAT MY SON HAS ARRIVED SAFELY AND HAS MADE CONTACT. WE WOULD HAVE PREFERRED THAT A YOUNG CIVILIZATION SUCH AS YOURS COULD HAVE REMAINED IGNORANT OF THE EXISTENCE OF

THE OUTER GALACTIC ALLIANCE UNTIL YOU
HAD ACHIEVED THE NECESSARY STANDARDS
OF SCIENTIFIC AND SOCIAL DEVELOPMENT,
BUT THAT WAS NOT TO BE."

There was a moment of silence. Alex turned to Sus. The
alien was staring at the circle of light.

"THE PRAYERS OF OUR PEOPLE ARE WITH YOU,
PEOPLE OF EARTH, AS YOU ARE THRUST INTO
A WAR NOT OF YOUR CHOOSING. SUS, MY SON,
THE BLESSINGS OF MYSELF AND THE COUNCIL
ARE WITH YOU...WHATEVER THE RESULT MY
PRIDE FOR YOU SWELLS WITHIN MY HEART.
FAREWELL."

The circle of light suddenly vanished. Sus extended his
hand. The small pearl sphere once more was resting in his
open palm.

CHAPTER 17

A STUNNED SILENCE FILLED THE ROOM. Mr. Dickson turned toward Rick James. "Do you believe him now?"

The reporter turned to the cameraman. "Did you get all of that, Fred?" The cameraman, his eye on the viewfinder, nodded his head. "I'm just playing it back, Rick...It's all there..." He lifted his head and gave a nervous grin. "This is going to blow their socks off."

Mr. Dickson stepped up to him and took hold of the reporter's arm. "Do you believe Sus?"

"Yes...yes, I believe him. I've covered some wild and crazy stories before, this one I believe." He turned to the cameraman. "Let's go, Fred." He took hold of the door handle and pulled it open. Fred stepped past him into the night. The reporter started to follow.

"Wait!" Sus walked up to the reporter. "You cannot show my father's message to all the people. It would only result in disorder."

The reporter stared at Sus in disbelief. "This must be the greatest story of this century, maybe any century. The people must know, Mr. Sus."

"They will eventually know, but not yet. Your leaders must

have time to make plans to defend your world, but time is short. Don't you see? "

The reporter stared at Sus in silence for some moments. He let out an audible sigh. "You're right of course." He turned to the others in the room. "We will get this to the proper authorities."

"Will you let us know what's happening?" said Mr. Dickson.

Rick James nodded. "I will probably be doing a piece about the strike on the eleven o'clock news. If I have a handkerchief in my top pocket you will know that all is well." He gave Sus a final look, shook his head slowly and stepped outside into the night.

Mr. Dickson turned to Fiona. "Ask your mother to call Dr. Bruce and get him to come over right away." Fiona ran outside. There was a commotion behind Alex. Sus had slumped further down in the seat. Mr. Dickson turned to Alex and Jim. "You lads give me a hand to carry Sus to the manse." As they eased Sus through the narrow outside door, the sound of a car engine starting up, and the scrambling sound of speeding wheels, marked the speedy departure of the TV crew. They reached the manse and carried Sus through to the living room. As they placed him on the large, leather settee, Mrs. Dickson and Fiona came in. "Dr.Bruce will be here in a few minutes," said Fiona.

The tick tock of the grandfather clock and the crackle of the logs in the open fireplace had a calming effect on the turmoil in Alex's mind. The crunch of tires on gravel and the slamming of a car door gave notice of the arrival of Dr. Bruce. Soon he was leaning over Sus, applying his stethoscope to his chest. After a few moments he straightened up. "This man should go to the hospital."

Mr. Dickson shook his head. "That isn't possible, doctor."

Dr. Bruce gave the minister a startled look. "The man is very ill."

Mr. Dickson rubbed his forehead with his hand. He looked at Alex and the others before turning back to the doctor. "Let's go into my study...I will explain." He turned to his wife. "Why don't you put on the kettle for a pot of tea, Rose. The doctor and I will be back shortly." He took Dr. Bruce by the arm and ushered him out of the living room.

Mrs. Dickson cast a troubled glance at the alien as she left the room. Alex looked at his watch. It was almost 10:30 p.m. The events of the day had left him drained. He felt as if he was living out some weird dream and he would wake up any moment. He glanced toward the settee. Sus's eyes had opened. "What happened?" he asked in a low, husky voice.

"You passed out," said Alex.

"The doctor's been to see you," said Fiona.

Sus sat up and swung his feet onto the floor. "Did those two men take my father's message?"

"Yes...they got it all, Sus," said Alex.

Sus rose unsteadily to his feet. "Will your leaders see it? Will they act?"

Alex exchanged glances with Jim. "The reporter said he would make sure the right people saw it. Maybe even the Prime Minister."

Sus sat back own on the settee. "Will they come here?"

Alex shrugged his shoulders. "I suppose they would have to send somebody. You can't go to them."

Sus nodded. "I have something I must give to them."

Mrs. Dickson reentered the room. Her eyes lit up when she saw Sus. "You're feeling better then?" She went over and sat down beside him. "Would you like something to eat?"

Sus smiled. "To eat would be good…yes, good."

She nodded. "Just take it easy, and I'll bring you something." She quickly left for the kitchen. Sus leaned back and rested his head on the settee. He closed his eyes. Jim had switched on the TV and was clicking through the channels

Fiona spoke up. "The news won't be on till eleven. You might as well switch it off."

Jim shrugged his shoulders. "I suppose you're right." He turned to her. "Do you have any video games? It would take our minds off all this."

"We do," said Fiona. "They're in the TV table drawer."

Jim pulled open the drawer and pulled out the video console and two joysticks. "Who fancies a game?" He took a game cassette out of the drawer. "Here we are, 'Invasion Earth.' How about it, Alex?" He pushed the cassette into the slot and punched a button.

An electronic voice sounded out. "WELCOME DEFENDER…EARTH IS BEING INVADED BY THE ALIEN SPACE FLEET. YOU ARE THE LAST…"

Jim whistled in appreciation. "Boy, oh boy! This is the latest. It's just like the one they have at the Video Games Café." He took hold of one of the joysticks. "Okay, let me go first."

Fiona came beside Alex. She gave a nervous smile. "My dad bought it for me for my birthday," she smiled, "I think he would like to have had a son."

"Are you Okay?" Alex asked quietly.

She wrinkled her nose. "I was until Jim put on the game. It's just a bit too close to reality." She placed her hand lightly on his arm. "Truth is, I'm a wee bit scared."

Sus, who had been watching Jim, turned to Alex. "This game. It is the same as the one in the café?"

"Yes, except you play it through the TV." Sus nodded his head but did not speak.

The door opened and Mr. Dickson appeared. "Well, I'm afraid the doctor is too much of a rationalist to believe our story completely."

"Where is he?" asked Fiona.

"He had to go back to his surgery. He said he would be back later to check on Sus. He wants to take him to the hospital." He turned to Jim. " I phoned your mother, Jim, and told her you and Alex were with us. Given the lateness of the hour I suggested that you two could stay the night and she agreed. With all the strike unrest she was happy to hear you are safe inside." He smiled. "Of course, she was a bit curious about what was going on. I said I would tell her more about it tomorrow."

Mrs. Dickson arrived with a tray of sandwiches and a pot of tea. Mr. Dickson kept up a lively conversation, but as time passed he made frequent glances at the grandfather clock. Nobody seemed particularly hungry. The big hand inched its way up to the hour. Mr. Dickson stood up. "We better switch over to BBC." Jim exited the video game and clicked the selector until channel five appeared. The screen flickered into life. The station logo appeared accompanied by stirring music. Then the familiar face of the news anchor appeared. The smile that usually graced his handsome face was missing.

"GOOD EVENING VIEWERS. THIS IS BILL STARR WITH THE ELEVEN O'CLOCK NEWS." He shuffled some papers in front of him as he stared straight ahead.

"BEFORE WE GO TO THE NATIONAL AND WORLD NEWS WE HAVE A SPECIAL BULLETIN. RICK JAMES, OUR ROVING REPORTER FOR THE PAST FIVE YEARS, AND CAMERAMAN, FRED HILL, WERE BOTH KILLED IN AN AUTOMOBILE ACCIDENT ON THE A68 TRUNK ROAD THIS EVENING. THEIR FORD ESCORT WAS IN A COLLISION WITH A VOLKSWAGEN DRIVEN BY MR. DONALD McCRACKEN, A RESIDENT OF NEWBATTLE. MR. McCRACKEN ALSO PERISHED IN THE COLLISION. BOTH CARS WERE COMPLETELY DESTROYED BY FIRE..."

CHAPTER 18

A CHILLING CLOUD OF DEPRESSION HUNG over the manse. Mr. Dickson had gone to his study and Mrs. Dickson was in the kitchen. Alex and the others were sitting around the fireplace. Sus sat on the settee with Fiona beside him. He was deep in thought. Jim stood up and walked over to the coal fire, picked up the poker and jabbed at the dying embers. "What do we do now?"

Alex shrugged. "I don't know."

Sus stood up and crossed over to the window. He stood for some time watching the snowflakes drifting down outside. He turned to Alex. "What time is it?"

Alex looked at his Timex wristwatch. "Almost 11:30."

"At 1:00 o'clock, my craft will pass overhead."

"Will that be the last time?" said Alex.

Sus shook his head. "No…It will go into a lower orbit, which will bring it overhead two more times." He looked at the clock. "The last time will be 3:00 o'clock in the morning."

"What do you mean 'the last time?'" asked Jim.

"If the beacon does not activate, my craft will go into a larger orbit. Though its cloaking technology makes it virtually undetectable by your satellite systems, there is always some risk with repetitive low orbits."

"It will come back won't it?' said Fiona quietly.

"It will return Fiona, but too late for me."

The door flew open, bouncing against the rubber stop. Mr. Dickson strode in, hair disheveled, clutching two large books to his chest. He dumped them down on the table. A small cloud of dust rose up. His face was slightly flushed. "I have found some interesting information."

They all approached the table. Mr. Dickson picked up the largest and oldest looking book and blew off some dust. Its ancient looking leather covers were scarred and stained. One corner was scorched black. He opened it at a page marked with a scrap of newspaper. One page of the yellowed parchment was covered in Latin script, beautifully illuminated. On the facing page was a painted picture. Fiona gasped, "It's the same as the window, Dad." There was no doubt about it. The colors were somewhat faded, but it was the same as the stained glass window in the church. Jacob was sleeping with his head on a green colored pillow. In the background was a hill. There were angels descending and ascending the shining ladder between Earth and Heaven.

"Can you read Latin, Mr. Dickson?" said Jim.

"Not very well, and this was handwritten by a monk almost five hundred years ago." He picked up the other book. It was obviously not nearly so ancient as the first. "This is a local history book written by Reverend Carrick, minister here from 1850 to 1875." He tapped the Jacob's Ladder picture. "He has quite a lot to say about this. He was pretty good at deciphering the Latin and was able to piece together the story." Mr. Dickson started to pace the carpet. "The monastery was built during the reign of David the First. They built a wall along the boundary of the monastery property."

"The Monkland Wall?" said Fiona.

Her father nodded. "Exactly." He paused. "One hot summers evening, about five hundred years ago, one of the elder monks, Brother Mark, was having a sleepless night and he decided to take a moonlight stroll. He followed the path that ran along behind the Monkland Wall. It was well after midnight when he had reached the section just opposite where we are now. Then he saw something that nearly scared him out of his habit." He paused. "You have to understand that, in those days, this area was heavily wooded. Above the treetops he saw a light blue column of light pointing up into the heavens. Frightened as he must have been, he decided to investigate. He found a door that took him to the other side of the wall. The blue light was still visible and he set off toward it through trees. When he reached the lower slopes of the law, he could see that the light was originating from somewhere higher up. He set off along a path through the trees. As he climbed higher and higher, the trees began to thin out and be replaced with Scotch-broom and rough grass. He could no longer see the blue column of light. He staggered onto the summit, tired and a bit out of breath. All he could see in the cold moonlight was the circle of standing stones. But as he drew near to the perimeter of the circle he saw something. There, inside the stone circle, was a silver chariot."

"A chariot?" Fiona exclaimed.

"Well, that's what Brother Mark called it. But that was not all. He saw two men in silver suits. Brother Mark thought they were angels. Then he was spotted. The 'angels' ran toward the chariot and vanished. Suddenly the blue column of light streaked up into the sky. The silver chariot began to accelerate in a circular path around the shimmering column and began to spiral up into the sky. Petrified, Brother Mark fell on his knees, pulled his cassock over his head and started praying. When at last he summoned the courage to lift his head, the column of light, the chariot and the angels were gone. At first he thought it was all a dream, then he saw a faint luminous green glow in the ground at the center of the circle of standing stones. He slowly got back on his feet, and holding his crucifix up slowly walked toward the strange light. It was coming from a cylindrical object projecting several inches from the ground."

Jim gasped, "What did he do then?"

The minister sighed. "Old Carrick wasn't able to find out."

"Why not?" asked Alex.

Mr. Dickson turned to the older book and flicked over the page. A ragged strip of scorched parchment stuck out from the binding.

"Missing pages?" groaned Fiona.

Her father nodded. "I'm afraid so." He closed the book. "Later, the monks built a small chapel on top of the law and, at the same time, built St. Jacob's Chapel close to where Brother Mark had been standing when he saw the vision. It was just on the other side of the wall, opposite the present church. When the mob set fire to the building and demolished it, a few items were saved. This book was one. The baptismal fount was another. Not much, I'm afraid." Mr. Dickson picked up the second book. "I found out another piece of interesting information from the Reverend Carrick. The monks gave a name to the place where Brother Mark had seen his vision. 'Jacob's Ladder,' they called it, for obvious reasons. Over the years, the name altered. Jacob's Ladder became Jacob's Lawder, which in turn became Jacob's Law and finally..."

"Jake's Law!" said Fiona.

Her father nodded his head. "Exactly! Jake's Law. He turned to Sus. "The ladder of light that Brother Mark saw must have been some of your forefathers paying us a visit."

"What about the stone that lit up?" said Jim.

Sus nodded his head slowly. "The trigstone."

Mr. Dickson turned to Sus. "Why don't you explain to us all a bit more about the trigstone?"

Sus walked over to the settee and sat down. "You must understand that my people have been sending survey expeditions here since long before your recorded history began. We established beacon stations, such as the one on your hill, all over this world. It was customary for survey expeditions to visit your planet regularly and secretly observe the development of the world and its species. During this time, their craft would go back into orbit around Earth. These expeditions became more difficult as Earth's population grew. Every effort was made to ensure that our presence was never detected by the natives. To that end, an effort was made to limit the need to carry too much sophisticated technology with us as we travelled around your planet. In keeping with that policy, trigstones needed to summon down an orbiting craft were hidden in the vicinity of each beacon. Some of our beacon sites became places of superstition and centers of pagan religions. Later, some were marked out by circles of standing stones."

"You mean like on 'Stonehenge?'" asked Jim.

"And the 'Twelve Apostles' on Jake's Law?" said Fiona.

Sus nodded. "Yes, Fiona, and many others all over these islands. Then, as civilization developed and cities appeared, our visits became less and less frequent. The incident seen by the monk was one of the last survey groups to land on Earth.

They visited each of the beacon sites, starting in the south, and deactivated the trigstones."

"Destroyed them?" said Alex.

Sus shook his head. "No, no, they would only be removed for adjustment and then replaced in the switch cavities."

"What difference did that make?" asked Jim.

"If one of our spacecrafts passed over the beacon in a low orbit, it would cause the trigstone to glow and give out an identifying sound. It would also rise several inches out of the switch cavity. This helped our people find it. To call down a craft, all they had to do was to push down on the trigstone. Once they got on board and took off, the trigstone would sink down until it merged in with the natural terrain. When they were deactivated, they no longer glowed or sounded a signal when a craft passed over."

"Then why did the trigstone light up when Brother Mark was up on Jake's Law?" said Fiona.

Sus shrugged. "This was one of the final beacon sites to be visited by the survey group, but before they could deactivate it, they must have been disturbed and had to make an emergency departure."

"Because of Brother Mark?" said Alex.

Sus smiled. "Yes, most likely because of Brother Mark."

Mr. Dickson looked puzzled. "If the trigstone is not in place, how were you able to land?"

"Landing only required the trigstone to be somewhere in the vicinity of the beacon. However, to bring my ship back, I have to trigger the beacon from here. Otherwise it will stay in a wide orbit."

Mr. Dickson started to pace the floor. "What is the size and shape of the trigstone, Sus?"

"It is one foot long and six inches in diameter."

"Brother Mark must have taken it," said Fiona.

Sus looked at Fiona and then at the clock. "I have three remaining opportunities to bring my space craft down to Earth - 1:00 a.m. 2:00 a.m. and finally 3:00 a.m. Then, if the trigger does not activate the beacon, the craft will leave."

Fiona turned to Sus. "If we were near the stone at one o'clock, we would see it light up, wouldn't we, Sus?"

"Yes...you would see it glow...you would also hear it." He turned to Mr. Dickson. "The trigstone is in this area, otherwise I would not have landed at this beacon. I should have landed at the beacon closest to your capital city. This beacon is the only one still functioning."

Jim's brow wrinkled. "Why would that be, Sus?"

"Das was aware these beacons could be used by the Federation to send assistance to Earth. When he first arrived, his first task would be to put the beacons out of action."

"Why did they miss this one?" queried Jim.

"To deactivate the beacon, he would need the trigstone."

"Couldn't he use another trigstone?" said Alex.

Sus shook his head. "Each trigstone was specific for one beacon. They were not interchangeable."

"Das must have been looking for it all this time?" said Fiona.

Sus nodded. "That explains why he and so many of his people are in this area."

Jim sighed. "If he hasn't been able to find it in all this time, what chance have we?"

Sus turned to Jim. "I think the odds against finding it are great." He looked toward the grandfather clock. It was midnight. The chimes rang out. One...two...three... As the last one struck, a depressed silence fell upon the room. Sus put his hand into the pocket of his jacket and pulled out a small, oval shaped metallic box. He laid it carefully down on the table and turned slowly to face them all. "My friends, I now have only a few hours left." He placed his fingers lightly on the small box. "This technology was to be given to your scientists and military leaders to enable them to defend Earth against Tan's invasion fleet—to put them in control of the five fighter ships that are already closing in on Tan's fleet. If all had gone as planned, I would have been able to direct their use of our ships to destroy Tan and his fleet. That is now out of the question." He smiled, "The only people of Earth who believe me are you, my friends." He picked up the box. "With or without the trigstone, I will not be here when the fighter ships intercept Tan."

"What can we do Sus?" murmured Fiona.

"You must destroy Tan's fleet."

CHAPTER 19

A BEWILDERED SILENCE WAS AT LAST broken by Fiona. "How can we do that?"

Sus opened the lid of the box. "With these!" Held in place by a clear, spongy material were five small pearl like spheres. Sus picked out one of the spheres and held it in his hand. "Please switch on the game, Jim."

Jim raised his eyebrows. "He means the video game," said Fiona.

Jim went over to the TV set. The game was still hooked up. He switched it on. The screen flickered into life and the game titles appeared.

"INVASION EARTH..." The electronic voice sounded out. "WELCOME DEFENDER...EARTH IS BEING INVADED ..." The message continued on till the final command. "...WHEN YOU ARE READY PRESS THE START BUTTON."

Sus stepped forward and placed the small sphere on top of the video console. Alex waited for it to roll off the sloping console top onto the floor. It stayed in place. Sus picked up one of the joystick controls. Fiona gasped, "Look at the screen!"

The video game graphics had gone. In its place was the star pierced, velvety blackness of deep space. Sus waggled the joystick. A metallic wedge shaped object came into view. Sus moved the stick once more in the opposite direction. Several other wedges appeared further away than the first. Sus pointed toward the screen. "These are Federation fighter ships."

Alex gasped, "Do you mean you are controlling them from here?"

"Just one. Each device controls one of the five fighter ships." Sus held out the joystick. "You try, Alex."

"What if I bump into one of the other fighters?"

"That will not happen. Their deflector shields will prevent that. Please try, but do not touch the red button."

Alex took the joystick. He moved the stick cautiously to the right. Another fighter ship drifted into view. He moved the stick left. More fighters appeared. He centered the joystick and once more the screen was filled with the dark emptiness of space. "Hold it steady there," said Sus. "Now, press the red button."

Alex did so. He almost dropped the control as a ball of brilliant blue light streaked off into the distance. There was a brief flash of a distant explosion then darkness.

"What was that?" Jim gasped.

"Energy cannon," said Sus. "One shot will destroy any one of Tan's battle ships."

Jim stepped forward. "Can I have a try?"

Jim very quickly became quite adept at the controls, but grew overconfident and approached too close to another fighter ship. A flashing yellow light appeared on the screen and bleeping sound filled the room. The ship's deflector shield activated and the course corrected to straight ahead. Jim, somewhat chagrined, handed the control back to Sus.

Fiona was still puzzled. "Where are Tan's ships? All I see are stars."

"They are still some distance away, Fiona. The robot fighters should catch up within the next few weeks."

"Few weeks?" Fiona looked at Sus. "But you will be gone..."

Sus held up his hand. "Please listen carefully. When the fighters are within attacking range the devices will glow. Then you will have to get to your video console and place the device on it."

"There are five ships," said Fiona. "There are only three of us."

"You have your parents."

Mr. Dickson gave out a gasp of protest. "Hold on Sus! Rose and I aren't wired like the youngsters. There must be someone else."

"Who else?" said Fiona. "If we bring people from the village now, it just makes it complicated."

Her father frowned. "The other thing is we don't have enough video consoles."

Fiona tossed her head. "Oh, Dad! We can borrow some...or even buy them. I have twenty pounds in my savings account."

"I have fifteen pounds I saved for my holiday pocket money," said Jim somberly. "I could chip in some of that."

Fiona rolled her eyes. "Chip in some? It's to save the world, Jim. If we lose, you won't need any pocket money...there won't be any holidays."

Mr. Dickson intervened. "Let's not fight amongst ourselves. We need to work this out." He turned to Sus. "Would any type of video game console work?"

Sus nodded. "It will make no difference as long it can plays the 'Invasion Earth' cartridge and the controls are similar to this. The device will be able to adjust." Sus picked the pearl sphere off the console and the video graphics reappeared. He walked back to the table and placed the device beside the others in the box. He closed the lid and handed it to Alex. He moved over to the couch and sat down. He suddenly looked weary.

"Switch off the TV, Jim." Mr. Dickson looked up at the clock. It was just past midnight. He clapped his hands together. "Look here everyone, Sus has given us the means to take on this Tan fellow and his fleet. He can't do any more than that. Now we have to try and get him home...We must look for the trigstone. I know it's a long shot but it's the least we can do." He turned to Sus. "You said it must be close by Sus. How close?"

Sus slowly raised his head. "It may not be on Jake's Law, but it must be within a half mile radius of the beacon to have allowed my vehicle to land."

Mr. Dickson went to the bookcase and pulled out an ordinance map. He took it to the table and unfolded it. He turned to Fiona. "Get me the compasses out of your school geometry box."

Fiona left the room and was back in less than a minute. Her father took the compasses and, using the map scale, opened them out to half a mile. He stuck the point in the center of Jake's Law and carefully described a circle. The penciled circle covered a small part of the village including the church and manse. It also just took in McCracken's cottage and the Deil's Quarry. Fiona pointed at the section of the village that came within the circle. "Surely, if it was in the village, someone would have seen it."

Her father nodded. "You're right, Fiona. The same goes for the manse and the church. That cuts down the search area a little bit."

Alex voiced his thoughts. "If Brother Mark took the trigstone, he would take it back to the abbey. It could be still there."

"Not necessarily," said Fiona. "St Jacob's Chapel was built as a sort of memorial to what Brother Mark experienced that night. It makes sense that they would keep the trigstone there."

"But the chapel was destroyed," said Alex. "If the trigstone was there and survived the fire, it would go to the abbey along with the other stuff they managed to save."

Mr. Dickson interrupted the debate. "You both could be right, but it's a moot point. The abbey is well outside the circle. The trigstone may well have been there once, but not now." He glanced at Sus. "Maybe McCracken did find it."

Sus shook his head. "I don't think so. Das said that they had failed to find it. However, it would have been activated by when I first landed. "

"In what way?" said Mr. Dickson.

"It would light up… with a dull green glow," said Sus.

"If it was out in the open, wouldn't somebody have see it?" said Fiona.

Sus nodded. "There must also have been several occasions in the past when orbiting scout craft would have caused the trigstone to glow."

"I thought your people left for good in the twelfth century?" said Mr. Dickson.

"We have not landed on Earth since then, but we have sent surveillance expeditions at significant periods in your history. They would have been able to carry out a low altitude orbit without detection. However, there have been none since your last world war when your detection capabilities made such rapid progress."

Fiona wrinkled her brow. "So, apart from when you landed, the last time the trigstone would have lit up was over fifty years ago?"

Sus nodded. "Yes, Fiona. It is just possible that the trigstone is still laying out in the open area and has not been found."

Mr. Dickson bent over the map once more. "In the time we have left, we don't have the capability to cover the whole area. It's a real needle in a haystack situation." He straightened up, " The abbey is out of range. St Jacob's no longer exists. There is no written evidence of any kind. The old manuscript that was salvaged from the fire does not say anything about the trigstone, though that may have been in the missing pages." He shrugged his shoulders. "It's a very long shot, but given our time restraints, the summit of the law is our best bet."

"Don't forget the cottage, Dad." Fiona spoke up. "McCracken may have found it."

Sus nodded. "I am sure that they did not have it up until I landed, otherwise they would have deactivated the beacon. However it is possible they have it now." He paused for a moment, "I would like to take a look inside Mr. McCracken's cottage."

"What about Das and his gang?" said Fiona. "They won't just sit back and watch us stroll over there."

Mr. Dickson groaned. "I had forgotten about them. They will be watching our every move."

Sus rose to his feet and approached the table. "Das will do anything to prevent my warning from reaching your leaders. If any of you try to leave the village, your fate will be the same as the newsmen."

"Why don't they come here and finish us all off?" said Jim quietly.

Sus smiled and reached out a hand to grasp Jim's shoulder. "They will not do that unless they get desperate. If none of us can leave the village, they think they have won. There are very few of them. They do not want to do anything that would turn the spotlight on their presence. They will be content to wait till I die."

Mr. Dickson looked at Sus. "My dear chap, I appreciate you don't want to frighten us, but the truth is, once you have gone they will want to shut the rest of us up. You have provided us the means to defend ourselves against Tan and his fleet. I understand that trying to find the trigstone is like finding a needle in a haystack, but we need to at least try. If you succeed in returning home, then, even should we fail, we will still have the hope that you will eventually come back to rescue us." He turned to look at the others. "I don't want to sound too melodramatic. We are all scared, but we don't really have much choice." He gave a grim smile. "They do say that we Scots are lovers of lost causes."

Sus was silent for some moments. He allowed his eyes to roam over everybody in the room. "My friends, the odds against us are very great. I am a man of power and prestige on my world. Yet I have arrived here in weakness. But for you, I would have fallen into the clutches of my enemies." He brushed away a drop of perspiration from his temple. "Tan's attempt to invade this solar system is the dying spasm of a doomed cause. He may win this battle, but eventually the wrath of my father will sweep him away." He looked at each one of his listeners in turn. "The odds are against me returning home, but should that happen, I will make sure that the story of your gallant efforts is known throughout the Alliance Federation."

"Well, that's enough for speeches." Mr. Dickson cleared his throat. "We have half an hour left to set up 'Operation Trigstone.'"

CHAPTER 20

PLANNING AND PREPARATION FOR 'OPERATION Trigstone' was by necessity, brief. Das and his alien cohorts would obviously be keeping a close watch on the manse, so a diversion was necessary. Mr. Dickson and the less than enthusiastic Mrs. Dickson were to provide that. The trigstone search party would be made up of Fiona, Jim, Alex, and Sus. Mrs. Dickson had been reluctant to allow Fiona to go, but had to relent. Time was running out and younger legs would be better suited to reach the top of Jake's Law before the hour struck. Sus and Alex would investigate McCracken's cottage and Fiona and Jim would go to the summit.

The strategy started well. Mr. Dickson went out fussed around the car, opening and closing the doors. Mrs. Dickson stood on the front doorstep swapping meaningless chatter with her husband. Alex, Jim, Fiona and Sus slipped out the French window and through the gate in the garden wall into the field. Soon they were stumbling across the frozen furrows toward the white bulk of Jake's Law. Alex glanced back toward the church. He could still hear the Dicksons' voices, but there was no sight of anyone else. The night sky was pierced with shimmering stars, but a sharp, biting breeze blinded them with stinging particles of powdered snow. They kept as close as possible to hedgerows and dry stone walls that formed the boundaries of the patchwork of fields and provided some protection from the elements and unfriendly eyes. The positions of the field gates in the hedgerows prevented them from taking a very direct route. It was a relief to exit the last field and reach the open lower slopes of the law.

They all stopped for a moment, their labored breath rising to form a canopy above them. Alex pulled up his anorak sleeve to look at the luminous face of his watch. It was almost a quarter to the hour. The two teams split, Fiona and Jim set off up the path to the summit and Alex and Sus took the path along the lower slopes that led to McCracken's cottage. The plan was to rendezvous back at 1:30 a.m.

Alex and Sus arrived at the cottage with minutes to spare. It was in complete darkness. Alex pulled his flashlight out, pointed it up toward the dark bulk of Jake's Law and did three quick flashes and one long. Almost immediately a flickering of light responded from the summit. "Three dots, one dash… They made it, Sus."

"Three dots, one dash…what is that?

"Morse code…three short, one long is the letter v…Means we made it. V for victory."

Sus smiled. "I see." He looked at the pile of stone cores that were stacked against the end wall. He turned to Alex. "What time is it?"

Alex glanced down at his watch. "A minute to go." Time itself seemed to slow up as the hand clicked its way around the dial. Alex counted out the last few seconds. "…seven…six… five…four…three…two…one…" Nothing happened. There was no glowing rock, no sounds.

Sus strode toward the front door. "Let us look inside." Sus

put his hand on the doorknob. It turned and the door swung open. Alex cautiously followed as Sus vanished into the dark interior. "Can you find the light?" Sus called out from the darkness. Alex ran his fingers along the wall till he found the switch and flicked it on. He blinked as light flooded the room. The living room was just as he remembered it. There was a faint odor of pipe tobacco. Sus saw something in Alex's expression.

"What concerns you, Alex?"

Alex shrugged. "I'm just thinking about Mr. McCracken. I can't believe he is dead. I can't believe he was an alien."

"I believe that there was a real Mr. McCracken, Alex, probably a genuine UFO investigator. I also believe that he died some time ago."

Alex felt a chill run up his spine. "They took over his body?"

"No, but the process would result in the death of the original Mr. McCracken."

Alex stared at Sus in disbelief. "You mean for every one of Tan's people, somebody here has died?"

Sus nodded. "Yes. Some identities would cease to be useful. They would adopt another body that would be more suitable at the time." He crossed the living room and opened another door. He stepped inside. Alex followed cautiously behind. It was a very small bedroom. A single bed against one wall, with a bedside table and lamp. The other piece of furniture was an old chest of drawers. The walls were covered in cheap floral patterned wallpaper. There were no pictures or any other decoration, except a full-length mirror attached to the wall opposite the bed.

Sus looked puzzled. He went to the door and looked into

the living room. He turned to Alex. "Does something strike you as strange about this room?"

Alex looked around. "It a bit on the wee side."

Sus smiled. "Yes. As you say, wee." He looked at the mirror. "It would seem that Mr. McCracken was concerned about his appearance." He walked back to the bed and pulled open the drawer of the small bedside table. "What have we here?"

Alex looked at the object that Sus had taken from the drawer. It was a small, black, plastic looking object, the size of a matchbox, with two silvery buttons. "It looks like a remote control." He looked around the room. There was no TV, no radio. Sus pressed one button with his thumb. A faint humming sound filled the room. Alex turned to locate the source. It was the mirror. He let out a gasp. The reflective surface had taken on a pearly grey opaqueness. Sus walked over to the mirror. He stopped just a foot or so away from it and thrust his right hand toward the glass. His lower arm disappeared as if it had been plunged into a pool of water.

Sus smiled. "I think we have found a portal door." He stepped forward and his whole body disappeared below the surface of the mirror.

Alex cautiously reached out his hand to touch the mirror's surface. His fingertips disappeared. He quickly pulled them back. A hand thrust out of the mirror, seized his wrist, and with a strong jerk, hauled Alex into the mirror. He instinctively threw his free arm in front of his eyes.

"It is Okay, Alex." Alex lowered his arm. Sus stood before him smiling. Alex was in a small, dimly lit room. He felt as if he was taking part in a bizarre scene from <u>Alice Through the Looking Glass</u>. Sus handed him the small control device. "Press the other button, Alex."

Alex cautiously took hold of the small black object

and pressed his thumb down. Multi- colored lights broke up the darkness. One wall of the small chamber had been suddenly transformed into a large electronic screen. Strange, alphabetic characters flickered around the perimeter. Lines of light crisscrossed the screen. Tiny blobs of orange light travelled along the lines. Alex turned to Sus. "What is it?"

Sus appeared not to hear the question. His eyes were fixed on the screen. A digital keyboard had apeared in the lower right corner of the screen. Sus reached out and his fingers tapped out a rhythmic motion. The image on the screen suddenly shrunk and a very familiar outline appeared on the screen. Alex let out a whistle. "It's the British Isles." One particularity bright spot of light was travelling across the map. His fingers tapped out another pattern on the keyboard. More strange alphabetical characters appeared on the screen.

Sus straightened up. A throbbing sound filled the room. The light continued to accelerate across the screen. He grabbed hold of Alex's arm. "We must leave right now!"

CHAPTER 21

STANDING ON THE SUMMIT RIM of Jake's Law, Jim saw the flicker of light in the darkness below. Three short, one long. He pulled out his flashlight and responded in kind. He looked behind him. Fiona was already heading for the ruined chapel. He stuck the flashlight back in his pocket and jogged after her. He caught up just as they reached the crumbled walls and the minute hand on Jim's watch reached the top of the hour. They stepped through the arch doorway. An unblemished carpet of snow still covered the stone floor of the chapel. "We should look outside," said Fiona. They stepped back through the doorway and looked around. There was no sign of any green glow on the snow-covered summit, only the dark silhouettes of the twelve ancient standing stones surrounding them like a circle of silent sentinels.

"It could be hidden behind the standing stones," said Jim.

Fiona nodded. "Let's work our way around the rim beyond the circle. I'll head over toward the quarry and you go the other way." They split up and took off in opposite directions.

Fiona headed toward the edge of the summit that overlooked Deil's Quarry. She shivered as she walked, eyes scouring the snow covered ground. She looked up. The stars were rapidly fading from view. A bank of mist appeared to have settled over Jake's Law. She flicked on the flashlight and looked at her watch. It was now four minutes past the hour. She could see no green glow and the mist seemed to be getting thicker. Then she heard a sound from above. It was faint at first, more like a vibration inside her head. A dark shape stumbled out of the darkness toward her. It was Jim.

"Do you hear it?" asked Jim excitedly.

"Yes…what is it?"

Jim shook his head. The noise was now all around them. He put his hands over his ears. Fiona followed suit. A draft of warm air wafted down onto them. Something was coming down out of the sky. Something invisible displacing the mist as it descended. The gusts of hot air now whirled around them.

They crouched together, pulling their anorak hoods down over their faces. Then suddenly the sound died away. Jim opened his eyes. Then they saw it. A shimmering oval shaped object drifted overhead, like a giant balloon, its surface reflecting all around it, rendering it almost invisible. They stood for some moments, eyes fixed on the shimmering object. It was at least thirty feet long and over twelve feet high. It would have been virtually invisible, but for the rippling of the surface.

"It's a big balloon," whispered Fiona. "You can see right through it."

Jim licked his dry lips. It was like a giant clear balloon. The object drifted beyond the summit lip and sank out of sight. The youngsters slowly and fearfully edged their way to the lip. Below them was horse shoe shaped Deil's Quarry, cut into the lower slopes of the hill and the object had touched down on the quarry floor. A flicker of blue light swept across the rippling surface. The balloon turned a cloudy color and suddenly was gone, like a bursting giant soap bubble. The mist had begun to dissipate. The balloon had not been empty. A dull metal colored mushroom shaped object now sat on the quarry floor. The top part was like an upside down soup dish, with tiny blue lights rippling around the rim, resting on a cylindrical base. Then the dish shaped top slowly rose up revealing more base. The blue lights on the rim were extinguished. A dim figure stepped out of an opening in the base. Jim craned his neck to take another cautious look, "There are three of them now."

"What are they doing?" whispered Fiona.

"They are heading out of the quarry," Jim whispered. "They are going to the cottage. We need to warn Alex and Sus." Jim took off toward the edge of the summit with Fiona close behind. They jumped over the lip and began to scramble and slide down the snow-covered hillside toward the base of the slope. Both were on the verge of exhaustion when they stumbled through the bushes of Scotch-broom onto the pathway that led to the cottage. Jim stubbed his toe on a root and sprawled on all fours.

"Careful, you clod!" Fiona hissed the words through clenched teeth. Jim, breathing heavily, scrambled to his feet. There was a sound of breaking twigs. They both froze. Then the muffled crunch of stealthy footprints and the branches of a nearby bush began to rustle.

"Jim! Fiona!"

Fiona let out a loud gasp of relief, "Alex?" The bushes opened up and Alex stepped out onto the path with Sus right behind.

Fiona grabbed Sus by the arm. "A UFO landed in the

quarry, Sus. Three people came out. We thought they would find you at the cottage..."

Sus put his hand on her shoulder. "We know Fiona. With McCracken gone, they probably have come to remove any evidence from the cottage. We got out before they arrived, but they may have detected our presence. We must get away from here."

"We saw no sign of the trigstone," said Jim. "What about you?"

Sus shook his head. "It was always a long shot. Now we have to get you back to safety."

A few minutes later, they had passed through the first field gate and were stumbling their way across the frozen furrows toward the lights of the village. A chilling wind swept across the open field. Alex kept looking over his shoulder, but there was no sign or sound of a chase. Or so it seemed. As they reached the second gate, Sus stopped and turned to look back toward the white bulk of Jake's Law. He leaned his head to one side, listening. "Do you hear that?" he whispered.

Alex shook his head.

Sus pointed toward the law. "See!"

Something was rising above the summit, a dish shaped object. It hovered for a moment and then skimmed down, following the slope of the hillside, heading straight for them. Sus shouted. "The wall. Get close to the wall. Run! Run!"

Alex took hold of Fiona's arm and in a crouching run headed toward the edge of the field. They reached the shelter of the stone wall first, with Jim and Sus just a few steps behind. They all crouched down, backs pressed hard against the wall. A nearby oak tree provided some very welcome extra cover from the moonlight. They started to edge their way along the wall. Sus took up the rear, eyes scanning the sky above.

"Stop! Down! Keep down!" Sus's warning sent the three youngsters diving for cover. A waft of warm air swept around them. Alex looked up. A giant disc shape was drifting across the sky overhead. He realized he was holding his breath. He let it out slowly through pursed lips, eyes still fixed on the alien craft. Suddenly a narrow beam of blue light pierced the night. A section of the wall next to Alex exploded into dust. He fell back, clutching his eyes. Someone grabbed hold of him and dragged him to his feet.

"Run! Run!" It was Sus. Alex started a stumbling run. Sus took hold of his elbow and helped him along. Another brilliant beam of blue light streaked overhead. A tree branch burst into flame.

"Through the gate," Fiona shouted. There was the scrape of rusty metal as she pulled back the bolt and the gate creaked open. They scrambled through; their faces reflected the flickering flame of the burning tree. Fiona started running alongside the wall, keeping her head well down. The rest followed. They had gone almost a hundred yards when Fiona tripped and fell to the ground. Jim tried to jump clear but his toe caught her shoulder and he also was sent sprawling. Alex and Sus pulled Fiona and Jim back up. Sus held up his hand. "Stay still. Do not move." He crouched close to the wall. The others followed suit, all breathing heavily, frightened eyes sweeping the sky.

"What is it, Sus?" Alex whispered. "Shouldn't we keep moving?"

Sus shook his head slowly. "They can detect us easier when we move." He raised his head to look over the wall. "The burning tree may concern them. They don't want to be seen by people in the village. As soon as the flames die down they will be back, but there is something I do not understand."

"What?" asked Alex.

"They have heat sensing equipment, but that has limited range." Sus took another peek over the top of the wall. "They came straight toward us. There must be something else that is leading them to us."

A loud cough sounded out from the darkness of the field before them. Fiona jumped to her feet, staring in the direction the sound had come from. There was another cough, nearer than the first. Something dark moved across the white blanket of the snow-covered field. Then another dark shape appeared, then two more. Alex's neck was stiff as a board. He tried to swallow but his dry throat wouldn't allow it. There was little room for escape; the dark shapes had already virtually surrounded them. Fiona gave out a quiet sob. Alex reached out and took her gloved hand.

Baa!baa!baa!baa!

Fiona let out a high-pitched squeal of relief. "Sheep! It's sheep." The now recognizable shaggy outline of a sheep had approached to within twenty feet of where Alex and the others were crouching. Alex turned to look for Sus. He was staring back the way they had come. The tree was no longer burning and a column of silvery grey smoke drifted up into the sky.

Sus turned quickly. "Alex! The control device from McCracken's cottage. Do you have it?" Alex stuck his hand into his anorak pocket. His fingers closed around something. He pulled it out. It was the control device. Sus grabbed it, threw it to the ground and raised his foot, then hesitated. He bent down and picked up the device. He stood up and turned to Alex, fixing his eyes on him. "My friend, please listen, we have little time...I must leave you now." Alex, puzzled, began to question but Sus cut him off. "Please do what I say. The future of your world depends on you all staying alive."

"What do you mean, Sus?" said Fiona, her voice trembling slightly.

Sus turned to her. "Regardless of what happens Fiona, I will not see tomorrow's sunrise." He looked at them each in turn. "There is something I can do now which may save you. The odds are not in our favor, but they are better than the alternative."

"What is that?" Alex said quietly.

"The certainty that we will all be dead within the next few minutes."

Alex, Fiona, and Jim exchanged nervous glances. Alex turned to Sus, trying hard to control the cold fingers of fear that clutched at his heart, "What are you going do?"

Sus held up the device. "They are tracking us with this. I will try to lead them away from you. Stay close to the wall and remain still until the right time."

"When will that be?" asked Fiona.

Sus gave a grim smile. "You will know, Fiona." He turned to Alex. "Take the shortest route to the village. They will expect you to be heading straight for the church." He looked toward the burning tree. The flames had died down considerably. "When the fire goes out, they will return." He turned to look at the handful of curious sheep that remained close by. He turned back to Alex and the others. "You must promise me that whatever happens, you will get to the manse and stay there."

Fiona moved in and put her arms around his neck, tears running down her cheeks. "Oh, Sus!"

Sus gently loosened her arms from around him. "I must go now." He looked quickly at each in turn, and then started to walk toward the sheep. The animals lifted their heads, then started to move away, heading back toward the main flock in the center of the field. Sus, arms stretched out wide, followed close behind. He started to walk faster. The now nervous sheep began to run.

Alex suddenly understood Sus's plan. "The wall! Get to the wall." He grabbed hold of Fiona and Jim and dragged them back with him. A gust of warm air wafted across them. Alex looked up. A dark disc shaped shadow passed overhead. They flattened themselves against the wall, oblivious to the sharp, cold, stones as their eyes followed the shadow of the silent craft, drifting ominously across the stars.

Agitated bleating drew Alex's attention back down to earth. Sus was still walking, arms outstretched, surrounded by an increasingly restless flock of sheep, he and they, now dark shadows against the white snow. Alex glanced up again. The disc was about one hundred feet above the ground and heading straight for Sus and the sheep. A streak of thin blue light lit up the night. A chilling animal squeal rent the air. More pencil thin blue rays streaked down from the disc. Panicking sheep scattered in all directions, their terrified bleating increased in pitch and volume. Deadly blue tracers of light struck one after another of the terrified creatures. Sus was still there, arms outstretched, steadily walking through the confusion, his figure lit up by each streak of light, creating the flickering effect of a horrific silent movie.

Alex tore his eyes away from the scene. "Run! We must run like Sus said." He pulled Fiona up and they started to run alongside the wall with Jim in close pursuit. The lights of the village seemed far away. The sounds of bleating, terrified sheep floated through the night air, but Alex forced himself not to look back. Fiona stumbled but kept running. The streetlights of the village seemed to be no closer. Suddenly, a bright light appeared in the sky ahead. A pulsating, throbbing sound filled the air. Alex stumbled over a rock. Jim, still looking up to the sky, collided with Alex and Fiona, and all three tumbled to the ground.

Alex lay on his back, his ears throbbing with deafening sound, a blast of air flattening him against the frozen ground, awaiting the blue beams of death to rain down. There were no blue rays. Alex rose up on his elbows. The pulsating, throbbing, thrashing sound was fading. The light in the sky was moving away from them. He now recognized the sound, "It's a helicopter." The three youngsters slowly rose to their feet.

"It's heading for the coal mine," said Jim. "It must be the police."

Fiona was scanning the sky around them, "The UFO has gone." She turned to Alex.

"The helicopter must have scared them off."

"Or it has done that invisible trick again," said Jim nervously.

Alex looked toward the center of the field. There was no sign of movement. "Sus told us to keep moving. I think we should run for the village." Without further ado, the three youngsters set off stumbling across the frozen field toward the safety of the village lights. They reached the first row of miners' cottages and set off along the narrow lane that accessed the rear gardens. The distant sound of police sirens drifted through the night. They headed toward the church, hugging close to the continuous brick wall that ran behind the gardens. They slipped though the gate into the manse's garden and ran to the back door. Fiona gently lifted up the iron doorknocker and gave it two light taps. There was the sound of approaching footsteps from inside.

"Who's there?"

"It's us, Dad. Quick! Let us in."

The door flew open and they all blinked as the hall light spilled out into the darkness. An agitated Mr. Dickson quickly ushered them in and quickly closed and bolted the door behind them. Mrs. Dickson came rushing down the hallway and gave Fiona a hug. "Your dad and I have been worried sick."

"Is Sus here, Dad?"

"No he's not!" Mr. Dickson retorted. "What happened?"

Fiona cast a quick glance at Alex and Jim before responding. "Quite a lot actually...."

Mrs. Dickson intervened. "They are frozen to the bone Stuart. Let's talk about this in the living room."

A short time later, they were sitting close to a blazing coal fire. The therapeutic combination of its flickering warmth and the hot tea provided by Mrs. Dickson had a calming effect on the traumatized youngsters. They quickly described what had happened since they had set out on "Operation Trigstone." Fiona's parents listened with growing concern. But, when they reached the part describing Sus's diversion plan to allow others to escape, Mr. Dickson jumped up. "We need to find Sus. He may be still alive."

"He made us promise not to leave here, Dad," said Fiona.

Her father walked over to the sideboard and took a large flashlight out of a drawer. "I understand, but he may be laying injured out there. I need to at least try."

"You don't know where to look," said Fiona. "We need to show you."

Alex stood up. "I will go with you, Mr. Dickson."

Minutes later, Alex and Mr. Dickson set off across the fields. Each carried a flashlight, but they were not switched on. The snow on the ground provided reasonable visibility. The night air seemed even colder than ever. Alex's face was numb. They passed through a gate and entered the field. There were no sheep at the feeding troughs, which were set up in sheltered positions close to the wall. As they cautiously neared the area where he had last seen Sus, a sense of foreboding had gripped his heart. Then he saw a dark shape on the snow. It was a dead sheep. They found more with each step in a variety of positions, no sign of blood, but all very dead. It looked like a battlefield, wooly bodies scattered all over. Then they found Sus. He lay flat on his back, his arms outstretched just as Alex had last seen him. Mr. Dickson shone his flashlight on his face. The eyes were closed. There was no breath condensing in the chill night air. Mr. Dickson knelt down, pulled off a glove with his teeth and placed his fingers on the alien's neck. He sighed and looked up at Alex. "I'm afraid he has gone, Alex. Sus is dead."

CHAPTER 22

The muffled sound of thE grandfather clock struck two o'clock two floors below. Alex's sleepless eyes stared at the centuries old attic roof beams. He had tried counting sheep but the events of the past eight hours continued to churn around in his thoughts. The camp bed creaked as he raised himself up on his elbows. The blanketed shape on the camp bed alongside was motionless. Jim was snoring gently. In the bedrooms on the floor below, the Dickson family was asleep. Alex swung his feet onto the cold linoleum. He tiptoed over to the dormer widow and drew back the lace curtain. The white cone shape of Jake's Law stood out against the dark evening sky. He looked back toward the front of the church. The sleek shape of the police Rover was parked on the grass verge across the road in the shadow of the Monkland Wall. The occasional glow of a cigarette end inside the car was a comforting indication that the officer Sergeant Brown had assigned was still on duty.

The body of Sus lay in the church on the communion table covered with a white sheet. The strike violence had swamped the ambulance services and Dr. Bruce had to arrange for the first available one to pick up the body. Someone moved

160

behind him. It was Jim. "What's happening?" he said hoarsely, his knuckles rubbing both eyes.

"I couldn't sleep. Did I wake you up?"

Jim yawned. "Maybe you did. Just as well. I was having a bad dream."

"You didn't look as if you were. You were snoring away in good style."

Jim shook his head. "Talk about the pot calling the kettle black. The last time you stayed over you were twitching around all night."

Alex shrugged. "I've got 'restless leg syndrome.' I don't do it all the time."

Jim gave a gasp and pointed out the window. "Hey! Look at that."

Alex turned to look. There was a flickering red glow appearing above the trees. "It might be the pit. It looks like a fire. It's in the right direction. I wish we could get a better view."

"I know the very place," said Jim. "The church bell tower. There's a ladder at the back of the pulpit. We would get a great view from there."

Alex thought of the body lying on the communion table. "Och! I don't think I'll bother. We might wake up the Dicksons."

"They were so beat, they wouldn't hear a bomb go off." Jim started to pull on his jeans. "Let's go before the fire goes out."

"What about Das and his guys?"

Jim shook his head. "I don't think they will be back now that Sus is dead...and the police are out front."

They quickly pulled on their clothes and soon they were walking toward the vestry. They kept to the shadows, out of the view of the police car. The door had been left open.

They slipped inside and walked through into the darkened sanctuary. Their footsteps echoed on the cast iron grating as they walked down the aisle. The illumination from the outside streetlamps diffused through the stained glass windows cast an eerie mosaic on the sheet-covered body lying on the communion table. Alex averted his eyes as he passed close to it to mount the pulpit steps behind Jim. They stepped through the small gate that gave access to the private balcony box behind the pulpit that once had provided reserved seating for the marquis and his family. Jim flicked on his flashlight. The balcony was only ten feet square, the internal size of the tower. There were several large wooden chairs, each with thick, dark red, brocade cushions. The balcony rail was in the form of a shelf and several large, leather bound, dust covered Bibles lay on it. Jim banged a cushion and a cloud of dust drifted into the flashlight beam. "At least their noble bums wouldn't go numb during long sermons, eh?" He turned the beam toward the corner. "There's the ladder." It was bolted directly to the wall and provided access to a trapdoor in the ceiling twenty feet or so above them. Jim turned his flashlight beam on the ladder. "You go first."

Alex stepped on the ladder and started to climb. He reached the trapdoor and took hold of the rusty bolt that held it down. It was stiff, but it slid back at first pull. With the flat of his hand he pushed up on the trapdoor. He flinched as a blast of cold air struck his face. He hauled himself up through the opening, taking care to lay the trapdoor back gently. Jim, right behind him, poked his head above the rough wooden floor. He clicked off his flashlight and climbed up alongside Alex. He shivered as he jammed the flashlight into the back pocket of his jeans. "Boy! It's like the North Pole up here." The large bell hung motionless in its trestle. They eased their way past it to one of the arched wooden slated openings that were on all four sides of the tower.

The space between the slats was quite large. By pressing their faces against the wooden frame they got a good view of the surrounding area. The icy swirling breeze stung Alex's face as he looked toward the red glow on the horizon. The giant, motionless, pithead winding wheels showed up clearly in the flickering red and yellow light of the flames.

"It's the coal mine," said Jim.

Alex nodded. "It must be one of the big storage sheds." The faint sound of a fire engine siren drifted through the wind. The flames were rising higher into the night. Alex let his eyes rove over the patchwork of hedgerows and fields laid out below. The whole village was visible and the white slopes of Jake's Law were tinged pink by the reflected light of the fire. Alex glanced at his watch, 2:15 a.m. Sus's ship would be passing overhead soon.

The silence of the night was broken by the whine of a car starter motor. He moved across to the other side of the tower. Down in the street, the police car's lights flicked on and the engine roared into life. A fine stream of sparks followed the trail of the cigarette ejected from the window. The Rover swung off the road and raced off up the hill.

Alex turned to Jim. "The police just took off."

Just then a sound came from the darkness below. Alex looked down through the slats. A small figure had exited the manse front door and was heading for the rear of the church. "It's Fiona."

Jim sniffed. "Any minute now she will start shouting and wake everybody up."

Alex blinked his watering eyes. "I've had enough up here. I'll go down."

Jim looked back toward the distant red glow. "I'll stay up here for a bit...The flames are getting bigger." Alex worked his way back around the bell trestle to the trap door. He scrambled down the ladder.

When he reached the vestry, Fiona was already entering. She seemed annoyed and a bit nervous. "What are you two up to?"

"There's a fire down at the pit. We went up the tower to get a better look." He gave her an apologetic smile. "Sorry if we woke you up."

"Well, you didn't. A phone call from the ambulance men did."

"What did they want at this time of night?" said Alex.

"They said they were coming for Sus. They wanted to know where he was. I didn't wake up Mum and Dad. They were both exhausted last night."

"I thought Dr. Bruce would have told them where Sus was?" said Alex.

Fiona nodded. "I'm sure he did. Must be another ambulance crew."

"How did you know we were across here?" said Alex.

Fiona ran her fingers through her hair. "After the call, I went up to your room. You weren't there and when I looked out the window, I saw your flashlight up in the bell tower."

Alex nodded. "I suppose we should hang around till the ambulance men come. We can let your Mum and Dad sleep."

They slowly walked down the aisle. Fiona stopped in front of the shrouded figure on the table. She reached out and took hold of Alex's arm. "What's going to happen to us? What's going to happen to everyone?"

Alex awkwardly put his hand over hers. "We'll be okay, Fiona."

Fiona straightened up. "Of course we will..." She cleared

her throat. "Just to be sure though..." She sat down on the front pew and pulled Alex beside her. He was somewhat taken aback and his expression must have shown it. Fiona sighed. "Relax. I'm going to pray."

"Pray?"

"What did you expect? My dad's a minister after all," she sighed. "And don't worry, I'll be brief." She reached out and clasped Alex's hand in hers. She closed her eyes and lowered her head. Alex followed suit.

Fiona launched into prayer. "Dear Jesus, you know the situation. You say that where two or three are gathered in your name, you will be there. We need you right now...Amen."

Alex opened his eyes. "That was brief."

Fiona shrugged. "He already knows what we need before we ask. We don't need to babble on."

"Then why bother praying?"

"Because He wants us to. It's polite to ask after all ...and you can let my hand go now." Alex dropped her hand as if it was a hot potato. He started to stand up. Fiona grabbed his arm and pulled him back down.

"What are you doing Fiona?"

"Listen! Can't you hear it?" There was a slight tremor in her voice.

Then he heard it. A strange whispering sound. Suddenly it increased in pitch.

Fiona's nails bit painfully into his arm, her eyes grew wide with fear. Alex turned in the direction of her gaze. A tall, cloudy, twisting shape was drifting out of the darkness towards them. He jumped to his feet. Something hot and wet brushed against his face. He staggered backwards. His leg struck the edge of the pew seat, he lost his balance and tumbled to the floor— taking Fiona with him. As he fell he heard her scream out, "The Monk! The Grey Monk!"

CHAPTER 23

ALEX, SLIGHTLY DAZED, SLOWLY SAT up. The whispering sound had gone. The Grey Monk had vanished. He looked for Fiona. She was sitting on the floor and rubbing the back of her head.

"Are you okay?"

"I'm fine! I'm fine!"

Then Alex noticed a faint bubbling noise. He slowly got to his feet. It was coming from the baptismal font. He stepped closer. The water in the bowl was bubbling gently. A thin plume of steam drifted up into the darkness of the ceiling. The bubbling ceased. Alex leaned over to look into the bowl. A faint wisp of condensation curled up from the now still surface of the water. Fiona came alongside. She dipped her finger into the water and pulled it out quickly. "Gosh! It's really hot." She turned to Alex. "What's going on here?"

"That was no ghost Fiona. It was just steam. The water in the font was boiling."

Fiona's brow wrinkled, "Steam? How can that be? It's made of stone! It's not an electric kettle."

There was a screech of brakes outside, then footsteps on gravel, followed by the creaking of the front door. Fiona reached out and grabbed Alex's hand. The inner door swung open and two shadowy figures stepped into the sanctuary. A powerful flashlight beam pierced the gloom, sweeping to and fro across the sanctuary, then coming to rest on the two youngsters.

"What are you kids doing here?" The voice was gruff.

"My father's the minister," Fiona shaded her eyes with her hand. "Who might you be?"

The flashlight beam drifted away from the youngsters' faces. "We're the ambulance crew. We've come to get the stranger that died. Do you know where the light switches are, lass?"

Fiona moved quickly to the rear pew, next to the vestry door and flicked a couple of switches. Ceiling lights instantly bathed the sanctuary in a muted yellow light. The two men spotted the covered body. "Ah! Here we are," said the one closest to the table, switching off his flashlight.

Both men wore dark blue uniforms and caps. They were carrying a trolley stretcher between them. They lowered the wheels and rolled it up alongside the communion table. They pulled the sheet off Sus and lifted him onto the stretcher. One man seemed familiar to Alex. The buttons on his uniform jacket seemed tight. They covered Sus with a blanket and adjusted belts to hold the body on the stretcher. A draft of cool air played on Alex's face. He glanced up toward the bell tower behind the pulpit. The trap door had opened. The two men straightened up. The one who looked familiar to Alex wiped his hands on his uniform. "Is it always so damp in here?"

Fiona gave Alex a quick glance. "Yes, especially in the winter." She took a step forward. "What are you going to do with him?"

The man shrugged his shoulders. "There has to be a postmortem. It's the law when somebody dies." He turned to look at Alex. His eyes were dark, like polished coal.

Then Alex remembered. He had seen him during the riot at the pit gates. He had been the one who had spoken to Sus and then called on the strikers to chase him. He was one of Das's men. The two men took hold of each end of the stretcher. As their gloved hands closed around the handles, Alex stepped forward. "I don't think you should take him just yet."

The tall man looked up. "What do you mean?"

Alex licked his lips. "Well, he is Dr. Bruce's patient. He should be here in a..."

The man slowly straightened up, his dark eyes bored into Alex's. "I don't think that is necessary, lad. The doctor can't do much for him now can he?" His lips curled into a humorless smile.

Alex gave Fiona what he hoped was a meaningful look. "Don't you think we should wait, Fiona?"

She was quick on the uptake. "Yes, I think we should call Dr. Bruce. It won't take long."

The ambulance man scowled. "Look, we've had a busy night and we can't hang around here any longer." He turned to the other man. "Let's go."

They bent down once more. Alex stepped forward holding out his hand. A gloved fist struck him full in the chest and he crashed backwards onto the hard stone floor. Fiona gave a shout and threw herself at the man. Alex scrambled to his feet. The tall man grabbed Fiona and threw her aside. Then the other man seized hold of Alex and forced him back against the base of the pulpit. The gloved fist drew back. Alex closed his eyes.

THUD! The grip on his shoulder loosened. Alex opened his eyes. The man was sprawled flat on his back, his cap brim crushed down over his eyes. On the floor beside him was a giant Bible. Alex looked up. Jim was leaning over the front of the pulpit giving thumbs up sign. His smile faded quickly from his face as the other man stepped over his comrade and started to climb the steps. Jim stepped out onto the top step. He looked around for an escape route. Alex ran up the stairs and threw himself at the man's legs. Jim pushed out with both hands. The man let out a startled shout as he fell back over Alex and tumbled down the stairs.

There was a sickening thump as his head struck the baptismal font. . It heeled over, hung in the balance for a split second, and then toppled to the floor. The crashing sound of stone against stone echoed around the sanctuary walls.

Alex ran down the steps. Both men lay sprawled on the platform, unconscious. Jim and Fiona joined him as he gave the two prostrate forms closer inspection. Jim cautiously poked his toe at the man who had been felled with the bible. There was no reaction. Jim smiled. "That put him to sleep faster than one of your dad's sermons, eh Fiona?"

She gave him a withering look and turned to Alex. "Who are they?"

Alex rubbed his shoulder. "I think they're Das' men."

Fiona turned away and groaned. "Oh no! The font...it's broken." They ran over and knelt down beside the damaged baptismal.

The font lay in two pieces. The top slab, with the bowl carved out of it, had broken free from the pedestal. Fiona shook her head. "Dad will go bananas."

Alex took a closer look. A circular peg of stone on the underside of the top slab had slotted in to a similarly shaped hole in the neck of the pedestal. The jarring fall had cracked the ancient mortar used to hold them together. He patted Fiona on the back. "It's not as bad as it looks. We can stick it together again." Alex rose to his feet looking at the two men. "I suppose there could be more of them outside."

"Could be," said Jim. "I saw that car with the yellow headlights parked around the corner. The ambulance stopped beside it before coming on to the church. I think Das is in it. We should get out of here right now before he comes looking for his pals."

Alex swallowed hard. "We need to get help. These guys will wake up soon."

They started up the aisle toward the vestry door. Fiona stopped at the last pew. "We should switch off the lights, it will slow them up a bit." Alex nodded and she flicked the switches. It took a moment for their eyes to adjust to the sudden darkness.

"What's that?" Jim's voice cracked as he spoke.

Alex followed Jim's pointing finger. A faint greenish glow lit up the pulpit and communion table. Fiona grabbed Alex's arm. "The font...it's the font." She ran back down the aisle with the others close behind. She stopped suddenly. Alex bumped into her. She stared ahead wide eyed. Her face was tinged with the gentle green light. It radiated from the hole in the neck of the pedestal. As they watched the light began to grow dimmer and dimmer. Darkness once more claimed the sanctuary, except for faint, distorted lights of the streetlamps reflected through the stained glass windows.

Jim looked baffled. "What is it? What's going on?"

Alex turned to him. "Just a wee while ago, we thought we saw the Grey Monk ghost, but it wasn't a ghost. A weird noise was coming from the font and the water was boiling. The 'Grey Ghost' was just steam."

Jim shook his head. "I don't understand."

Fiona pointed at his wrist. "Look at your watch. What time is it?"

Jim glanced at his watch. "2:35. So what?"

Fiona sighed. "Don't you see? It happened at 2:30."

Alex knelt down beside the font pedestal. He cautiously put his fingers in the round hole. The sides were smooth and warm. "Jim. Help me lift up the base." Jim handed the flashlight to Fiona and took hold of the stone base.

"Okay," said Alex, "at the count of three. One...two...three!" The base rose several inches clear of the floor. A sliding noise came from inside the pedestal and stopped.

Fiona let out an excited cry. "Something is there! Lift it higher." The boys strained once more. Alex could feel his pulse throbbing in his temple. The sliding noise began again. There was a loud clunk as something dropped onto the stone floor.

Fiona gave a squeal of triumph. The boys let the base crash to the floor. Alex blinked away the sweat from his eyes. The object that lay on the floor was about a foot long and six inches in diameter. The surface had the color and texture of dull green marble. Alex reached down and lightly touched it. It was still warm. He bent down and carefully lifted it up. It was lighter than he expected.

"It's the same as in the picture," said Fiona.

"What picture?" said Jim.

"Don't you see? The Jacob's Ladder picture in the old book." Fiona pointed to the stained glass window. "The same as that."

Alex looked up. Even in the poor light he could see what caused Fiona's excitement. The image of Jacob—his head was resting on a green rock. But it was not a rock. It was the trigstone.

CHAPTER 24

ALEX LOOKED UP TO FIND Fiona's eyes on him. "We still have time," she said softly. He glanced at his watch. It was 2.40 a.m.

"Time for what?" Jim looked quickly from one to the other.

"To send Sus home," said Fiona.

Jim's jaw dropped. "But he's dead, Fiona."

"If you died in some far away place, wouldn't your family want to bring you home?" She turned to Alex. "Surely you understand that, Alex."

Jim gasped, "How can you say that, Fiona? Tom died on the other side of the world, not the other side of the galaxy." There was an awkward silence. Alex's thoughts were elsewhere. Just a few days after the Watts family had been officially informed of Tom's death, he had heard a sound coming from his brother's bedroom. The door was slightly ajar. His father was sitting on the bed holding one of Tom's football shirts up to his face, sobbing quietly. Alex had slipped away before his father noticed him.

Fiona reached out and gently touched his arm. "Sorry, Alex. I didn't mean it to sound like that."

"It's okay. You're right, Fiona." Alex looked down at trigstone. "We should give it a try."

Jim let out a sigh of resignation, "How do we get Sus out of here without being seen by Das?" He tapped the face of his wristwatch. "And how can we get up to the top of Jake's Law in less than twenty minutes?"

Alex looked at the two unconscious aliens. "We can put on their hats and jackets and wheel Sus out on the stretcher. The street lights are pretty dim. Das might not catch on until we drive off."

"Drive off?" Jim's brow wrinkled. "In what?"

"The ambulance, Jim, what else?" said Alex.

"Who's going to drive?"

Alex shrugged. "Me! I drove Dad's car today."

Fiona clapped her hands. "Let's go then!"

Alex shook his head. "It might be best if you stay Fiona."

Fiona's eyes glinted. "Do you want me to have a pot of tea ready for when you get back?"

"It's not that! Das will expect to see only two people and someone needs to tell your mum and dad what's happened."

Fiona was silent for a few seconds. She shrugged. "I suppose you're right." She laid her hand lightly on his arm. "Be careful."

A few minutes later, Alex and Jim, wearing the ambulance men's hats and jackets, wheeled the stretcher trolley out of the front door of the church. Alex, glancing out the corner of his eye, spotted the dark shadow of a parked car just fifty yards ahead of the ambulance. Alex and Jim struggled for a moment to collapse the trolley wheels and slide the stretcher into the ambulance. The trigstone was at Sus's feet, covered by the blanket.

They climbed into the ambulance and pulled the door

closed behind them. They squeezed through the bulkhead door into the driving cab. Alex slipped into the driver's seat. He took out the keys he had collected from one of the unconscious aliens. As Alex inserted the key into the ignition, Jim climbed into the front passenger seat. He glanced down at the stubby gear stick. "You've lucked out. It's automatic. You just stick it into 'D' for drive." Jim's tone did not reflect the confidence of his words.

Alex slid the lever back into 'D' and turned the ignition key. Nothing. He tried once more. Still nothing. He swallowed hard. "The battery must be flat." He rolled the window down to get some air. Jim leaned forward and flicked a switch. The dash instrument lights lit up. Alex looked down at the gear stick. The illuminated gauge beside it read P, R, N, D. D2.

"'N' for neutral!" shouted Jim. He grabbed the gear stick and shoved it to 'N.' "Try it now." Alex turned the key. The engine roared into life. He pushed the lever into 'D' and pressed his foot down on the accelerator. The ambulance jerked forward. He hauled the wheel to one side, just in time to avoid collision with the parked car. He caught a brief glimpse of Das's startled face as the ambulance swung out into the center of the road. He glanced into his wing mirror. Two figures had staggered out of the church.

Alex pushed his foot down hard on the accelerator. The rear of the ambulance snaked from side to side as the spinning tires fought to grip on the ice-covered road. Suddenly, they took hold and Jim was thrown back into his seat as the ambulance accelerated off into the darkness. The roar of the engine echoed back off the Monkland Wall. Chill air stung his cheeks. He rolled up the window, glancing in the side mirror.

"BEND!" Jim's frantic shout brought Alex's eyes back to

the front. He hauled at the wheel and the ambulance skidded around the corner. The stone wall flashed by, desperately close. Now the ambulance was heading in a straight line down the dark corridor of the walled-in road. Jim slowly let out his breath. "Slow down before you kill us." Alex shot a glance once more at the side mirror. There was no sign of headlights in the darkness behind them. He eased up on the accelerator pedal. The streetlights of the outskirts of the village had appeared ahead. Jim cast a quick glance over his shoulder. "What road are you going to take?"

Alex, crouching forward over the steering wheel shook his head. "We need to drive up as far as we can go. There's only one way..."

Jim jerked his head back around. "Battery Road?"

Alex nodded. "It's the only way we can get there in time, Jim."

Jim took off the ambulance man's hat and ran shaky fingers through his hair, damp with perspiration. Battery Road had been constructed during World War II to supply the anti-aircraft installation on the summit. It was narrow and unpaved with precipitous drop offs. The icy conditions would make it even more perilous. Jim saw lights in the side mirror. Yellow headlights. "Faster, Alex."

"My foot is flat on the floor. I can't go any faster." He craned forward. They were approaching a bend. As the ambulance rounded the corner, the yellow headlights disappeared from the side mirror. An open field gate was coming up on the right. He flicked off the headlights and swung the wheel over. The ambulance skidded up off the road. Jim let out a yell, throwing his arms up to his face. There was the rasping sound of metal against stone as the ambulance scraped between the stone gateposts. Alex held on desperately as the ambulance bounced over the frozen furrows. "Sorry, Jim...short cut." He glanced back over his shoulder. His ploy had worked. Das's car was still heading toward the village. The snow-covered ground provided enough visibility to continue without the help of the ambulance's headlights. He steered straight, bouncing over the frozen furrows, straight toward the giant white cone of Jake's Law.

Jim, still somewhat shaken, looked at his wristwatch. "Almost fifteen minutes to go. We'll never make it." Alex did not reply. Then he saw the gap in the stone wall that bordered the field. The wooden gate was closed. Alex did not hesitate. The ambulance smashed through the timber as if it were balsa wood. They were now going over smoother ground. They had arrived at the lower slopes of the law. Alex drove around looking for Battery Road. Snow had begun to fall and flicked on the wipers. Then he saw the two old cast iron gateposts that marked the beginning of Battery Road. The gate and fencing had long since gone. He swung the ambulance through between the posts and headed on up the spiral road that climbed steeply into the darkness.

The snow was falling heavier than ever. The flakes were starting to cake on the wiper blades. Alex switched the headlights back on. The risk of being seen by Das and his men was far outweighed by the danger of driving off the treacherously narrow road as it circled up the slopes of Jake's Law. Alex was grateful to be able to hug the inner edge of the narrow dirt road.

Jim was still not comfortable. "Watch it. We're only a couple of feet from the edge." He took a cautious glance to his left and let out a mild groan, "Can you not move over a wee bit?"

Alex shook his head. "I'm right up against the banking

already." He glanced into the wing mirror. "Any sign of Das?" Jim wound down the window and stuck his head out into the swirling snow. A few flakes fluttered through the window as he craned his neck to see back down the steep slope. A cold draft of air disturbed Alex's hair. Jim pulled his head inside and quickly wound up the glass.

"Look out!" Jim's yelled out a warning. Alex foot jammed down hard on the brake pedal. The ambulance wheels locked. He pulled the steering wheel hard to the left and the ambulance skidded on the icy surface. The ambulance's front wheels struck the banking and then began to roll backwards.

"The brake!" Jim shouted, his voice high pitched with fear.

Alex grabbed hold of the hand brake and pulled it hard all the way back. The ambulance lurched to a halt. There was silence. The only sound was the creaking suspension of the still swaying vehicle. The engine had stalled. Snowflakes were building up on the windscreen. Alex stuck his head out of the window and looked back. His mouth went dry. The rear wheels were only inches away from the edge and the rear of the ambulance was hanging out over the steep slope.

Jim also stuck his head out then quickly pulled it back in. He turned to Alex, his eyes still wide with fright. "You just about killed us."

Alex snapped back. "You said stop."

Jim pointed a shaking finger out into the darkness. "Didn't you see the blooming rocks?"

Alex pushed open the door and stepped out into the chilled air. Snowflakes melted on his flushed face. He swallowed hard. Three big boulders were blocking the road just a few yards from where the ambulance had stopped. Alex turned as Jim came up alongside. "I didn't see them, Jim. Where did they come from?" He looked at the luminous dial of his wristwatch. It was less than ten minutes to the hour.

He ran over to one of the rocks and started to push it. Jim was right with him. The boulder slipped off the edge and rolled off into the darkness. They ran to the next rock and started to roll and drag it off the road. As it slid off down the slope, they turned to the third and last. It was less round than the others and more difficult to move, but their strength was increased by desperation and it rolled off into the darkness.

Alex turned quickly back toward the ambulance. He stumbled as his foot gave out beneath him. He looked down. There was a crack in the surface of the roadway. It was at least two inches wide. He had never seen cracks in the road like this. He followed the dark jagged line across the whole width of the road and for several feet up the slope. He turned to look back. Yellow headlight beams bounced across the grey darkness of the snow-covered ground at the base of the law. It was Das. "Let's go!" Alex shouted out as he jumped back into the driving seat, turning the key as Jim scrambled in beside him. The engine roared into life. He pushed the gear lever into drive and the ambulance's wheels began to spin, then bit into the surface and began to move up the road with ever increasing speed. Alex leaned forward, his eyes straining to see the road ahead through the sweeping wipers. Then there was a bone shaking thump, the steering wheel jerked violently to the left. The ambulance heeled over to one side and came to a jarring halt. The engine died. Alex jumped out. The front wheels of the ambulance had dropped into a large six-foot diameter hole that they had never seen before. They were on the top of Jake's Law, but the ambulance would take them no further.

Jim had jumped out of the ambulance and was staring at the hole. "What's happening? That wasn't here before."

Alex looked at his watch. It was three minutes to 3:00 a.m. "We have to carry him the rest of the way." He scrambled around to the rear of the listing ambulance and grabbed a hold of the handle. The heavy door swung wide. Jim was already pulling the other door wide open. They took hold of the stretcher and began to slide it out. A strange glow was coming from underneath the blanket that covered Sus's body. The trigstone was a dull, luminous green, growing brighter by the second.

Alex grabbed it and, clutching it to his chest, started to run across the uneven blanket of snow toward the dark outline of the ruined chapel. He could feel the heat building. He tripped and stumbled for a few feet but did not fall. He was only a few yards away from the chapel. The scorching pain in his hands was almost unbearable. He cried out in agony as he threw himself through the broken down arch of the doorway. A dark circle had formed in the snow on the floor of the chapel. He thrust the trigstone into the opening. A spasm of pain shot up each arm. The trigstone dropped out of sight. He buried his bare hands in the snow. The stinging pain in his fingers eased. He staggered to his feet and ran back toward the ambulance.

Jim had already pulled the stretcher halfway out. Alex took hold and together they lifted it clear. Jim reached for the release lever for the trolley wheels.

"Leave that, Jim." Alex gasped out the words. "It's too rough going for wheels, we'll have to carry him." Jim opened his mouth to protest. The words died in his throat as the ground beneath their feet began to shake. They staggered from side to side, fighting to hold their balance. Sus's left arm flopped out and swung like a pendulum. They both fell to their knees, still holding the stretcher. The ambulance suspension creaked as it rocked to and fro. A strange grinding sound filled the air. Alex caught a movement out of the corner of his eye. A speeding line of disturbance was tearing across the unblemished covering of snow, heading straight toward them.

CHAPTER 25

FIONA SAT AT HER BEDROOM window, eyes glued to her
father's binoculars as she scanned the cone shaped mass
of Jake's Law, barely visible through the falling snow.
When Alex and Jim had driven off, she had returned to the
manse. Her bleary eyed father met her at the door having
been awakened by the sound of the departing ambulance.
Fiona, still somewhat unnerved, breathlessly described the
incident in the church and Alex and Jim's desperate scheme
to send Sus home. As her narration reached its end, any traces
of her father's sleepiness had gone. He quickly dressed and in
minutes he was drove off in his red Mini toward the village
and the Police Station.

Fiona made sure all doors and windows were secure.
Her mother was still sleeping. Now, alone in her room, her
irritation at being left behind had transitioned into anxiety.
She lowered the binoculars and gently massaged her weary
eyelids. She raised the binoculars back up to view the summit.
There was something there. She twisted the focus to get a
clearer image and pushed the zoom lever. There were lights,
red rear lights and the small but unmistakable boxy shape
of an ambulance. Alex and Jim had reached the summit.

There was a flicker of lights lower down on the slopes of Jake's Law. Another vehicle was driving up Battery Road. The chill of fear clutched her heart. The headlights were yellow. Suddenly, a mild shudder shook her room. It was like a minor earthquake. Fiona jumped to her feet. Because of the long history of coal workings in the area, isolated instances of mining subsidence were not unusual, but this one seemed different. She focused the binoculars back on the summit. The red tail lights of the ambulance were still visible. Then, suddenly, they were slipping backwards. The lights appeared and disappeared as they continued to slide down the slope. The ambulance was tumbling down the law, heading straight for the advancing yellow headlights. There was a flash of orange flame and a glittering trail of sparks cascading down the slope and then darkness. She dropped the binoculars and ran out the bedroom door.

"Run! Run!" Alex screamed out as he scrambled to his feet. Knees buckling with the load, the two friends half ran, half staggered for several yards. A roaring sound filled the air around them. Alex felt the ground drop beneath him. A violent jerk painfully stretched the muscles in his arms. He was hanging in mid air from the handles of the stretcher. He twisted his neck to look back over his shoulder. A large section of rock was sliding down the slope and, with it, the ambulance. For a moment, the vehicle stayed on top as if it was riding a giant rock sled, then it tumbled off to one side. The violent sounds of colliding rock and metal rose up to him out of the darkness. A flash of orange light briefly lit up the night, followed by a muffled explosion, then darkness and silence. The wind blew icy particles on his face as he swung in mid air.

"Hold on Alex. Hold on." Jim's gasping words came from above. Alex craned back his head but could not see Jim, only the end of the stretcher. "Pull yourself up Alex...I can't hold it much longer. Jim's voice was strained with effort. Alex was heavier than Jim. It was Sus's weight that was helping them balance. Fear pumped adrenalin into his muscles. He swung to and fro, trying to find a foothold. On the third swing his right foot got a grip. He let go one hand and grabbed for the broken lip of rock above him. A hand seized the collar of his anorak. "Let go of the stretcher!" Alex instantly obeyed. His other hand found a hold and, within seconds, he was flat on his back beside the stretcher, his labored breath pluming up into the night air. Jim's white face appeared above him. "Are you Okay?"

Alex could only manage to nod his head. His arms trembled with the physical effort. He slowly sat upright. The snow had stopped. Jim cautiously looked over the broken edge of rock. "One good thing. The rock fall must have blocked the road. I can't see Das's car headlights." Alex jumped up and helped Jim pull the stretcher away from the edge.

A rushing, crackling sound filled the air. Alex wheeled around. A towering column of blue light had streaked heavenwards from the ruined shell of the chapel. As they craned their necks upward, they saw a flash of reflected light. The shining sphere was already spiraling downwards through the swirling snowflakes. It stopped for a few moments fifty feet above them, circled the beacon, and then recommenced its descent. Snow flurries whipped around them as the sphere touched down and gently rolled to a stop only thirty yards or so from them. The column of light had gone.

Alex bent down and seized hold of the front end of the stretcher. Jim grabbed the rear handles and they set off toward the sphere, as fast as their aching muscles would allow. They wearily shuffled to a halt several yards from the sphere and laid the stretcher on the ground. Both youngsters bent over with hands on knees sucking air into their winded lungs. Jim raised his eyes to look at the sphere. "We have a problem."

"What?"

"It doesn't have a door."

Alex slowly approached the sphere. There was no break of any kind in the mirror-like surface. Jim stretched out his hand, but his fingers stopped short of the surface. "There is something there that we can't see," he whispered.

Alex reached out his hand. A tingling sensation shot through his blistered fingertips. He had touched something solid, but there was a space of about two inches between the visible surface and his hand. A circle of rippling bluish light now distorted the mirrored surface of the sphere. The boys began to slowly back away. A faint humming sound now filled the air around them. A two-foot diameter opening had formed in the surface of the sphere. Something moved inside. A small cloud of luminous gas floated out into the cold night air. Jim groaned, "Not again!" Like spellbound rabbits, the boys stood, rooted to the ground, eyes fixated on the cloud floating toward them. As it swept in closer and closer Alex closed his eyes. Nothing happened. He opened his eyes. The cloud had disappeared. "Where did it go?" gasped Jim.

Alex slowly turned around. The cloud was now hovering directly over the stretcher. The pulsating blue light within it was getting brighter every second. An brilliant burst of white light flared up within the cloud. Alex threw his arm to shield his eyes. Then the light was gone. He cautiously lowered his arm. The cloud, still hovering over the stretcher, had returned to the faint, flickering blue luminosity of before. It started to float gently toward them. Alex flinched as the cloud drifted up within inches of his face. It stopped and hung there in mid air. A dull glow pulsed inside the cloud. The tension that had taken hold of his body drained away. Then the cloud drifted toward the sphere. It passed though the circular opening and vanished into the dark interior. Suddenly, the circle filled with the shimmering blue light and then it went dark. The sphere now stood silent and still. Its flawless mirrored surface once more restored, reflecting the falling snowflakes and the distorted images of the two boys. Alex started breathing again. He looked back to the stretcher. Something was different. He ran over and tugged the blanket away. There was no body on the stretcher. All that remained was the old army overcoat.

Jim came alongside and stared down in disbelief at the empty stretcher. "What's happened?"

"I think he is back in the sphere Jim, just like when he arrived."

"Then why isn't it taking off?"

"I don't know." Alex turned to look at the chapel. A green glow radiated out from inside the ruin, casting the jagged shadows of the crumbled walls far out across the white blanket of snow and made the snowflakes look like leaves falling from some heavenly forest. "The trigstone! We need to push down the trigstone." Alex began to run toward the chapel. Jim followed close behind. A blue ball of light streaked past him and an exploded against the chapel wall. Alex and Jim slithered to a halt.

"One more step and you both die." There was no mistaking the cold, menacing drawl. A dark figure materialized out of the darkness. It was Das.

CHAPTER 26

DAS WAS LIMPING. THE SOFT green light spilling out from the chapel cast a sinister hue on the sharp lines on his face. In his outstretched hand was a small metallic tube. He gestured with it. "I would like you both to move away from the chapel." They did not respond immediately. A small blue pulsating light shot from Das's hand and struck the ground in front of them. Alex and Jim jumped back. A dark patch, one foot in diameter, had appeared in the snow. "Quickly. It is not my desire to destroy talent, which can be molded into the service of Tan. Nevertheless..." Alex glanced at Jim. They began to slowly back away from the chapel entrance. When they where half way to the sphere, Das held up his hand. "That is far enough. Remain completely still."

His lips formed a mirthless smile. "You have achieved something where we failed. I must congratulate you. Given your youth and limited knowledge, you have shown capabilities and a gift of improvisation that can only benefit the Empire of Tan." He pointed toward the chapel. "You found the trigstone where we failed, but I'm afraid it has been too late."

"We just want to send Sus home," said Alex.

"I'm afraid I can't let that happen," Das had begun to move toward the sphere.

"Sus is dead. What difference does it make to you?"

Das shrugged. "That's true. Sus is dead, as you define the condition."

Alex stared at Das. "He could be brought back to life?"

Das now reached the sphere. "That would seem unlikely, however, we shall not take that chance."

Alex glanced toward the chapel.

Das seemed to read his thoughts. "Don't try anything foolish, my young friend."

Desperate thoughts raced through Alex's mind. Das was probably going to kill them anyway. One quick dash, just a few seconds, would take him to the trigstone. He edged in that direction.

Das raised his arm. "Do not try, young man." Alex took another step. A ball of blue fire hissed past his face. He froze.

Jim reached out and grabbed his arm. "Don't Alex. You'll never make it."

Das smiled. "Good advice, I think." He gave a quick glance up into the dark sky. A faint humming sound had begun to drift down through the falling snow.

Jim looked up and grabbed hold of Alex's arm. "It's the UFO, Alex." There was a tremor in his voice.

Das waved the weapon at them. "Move closer to the sphere, if you please."

Alex swallowed hard. "What are you going to do, Das?" His voice sounded more assertive than he felt.

"You are about to be part of history. The first of your species to join the service of Tan."

"We will never do that," said Jim.

Das sighed. "You have no choice, I'm afraid." He pointed

at the sphere. "You will accompany your friend, Lord Sus. I thought that would please you. He glanced at the sphere. We shall also take this vehicle and have its technology inspected by our scientists. We may then be able to restore Lord Sus. He will be a useful bargaining tool in our ongoing struggle with President Vah." As he spoke, the humming sound from above was getting louder and louder. Das looked toward the chapel. "Once we have you and the sphere on board our craft, we will remove the trigstone and destroy it. The crude tunneling and blasting your ancestors carried out have weakened the structural integrity of the hill and possibly the functioning of the beacon itself."

"The police will be here soon," Jim spoke defiantly. "They know we are up here."

Das sighed. "I do not think so. The road up here was swept away with the landslide. It took the lives of two of my men. I just managed to jump clear. Tomorrow, they will be found in the wreckage of my car and the ambulance. Just another puzzle to go along with your disappearance." The humming sound from above was getting louder by the second. Alex looked up. The shimmering silver disc was now visible, steadily descending through the falling snow, directly above and growing bigger every second. Das turned toward Alex and Jim. "The evidence in the cottage has been destroyed. We have Sus and the trigstone so there is no more reason to stay here. You are about to experience the journey of a lifetime."

Alex took a deep breath. It was now or never. He knew that the chance of success was negligible. He experienced a passing sense of elation. He wasn't afraid to die! He wasn't a wimp! But nobody would ever know. His dad would never know. Das was making more frequent glances up at the spacecraft. Alex whispered out of the side of his mouth. "Next time he looks up, I'm going to make a run for it."

Jim was silent for a brief moment. " We go together."

A blue bolt of light blasted into the snow just in front of them. "If you are thinking of making a rush to the trigstone, I would not recommend it." Das's weapon was pointing straight at them. "As much as I would prefer to recruit you into the service of Tan, one more step will result in your instant demise." He began to walk toward them.

Alex glanced up. The space craft had halted its descent and was now hovering about two hundred feet above them, directly over the chapel. Just then, he spotted something out in the darkness beyond the ring of standing stones. A figure had moved out from the shadow of the standing stones and had started running toward the chapel. Alex heart leaped. He recognized the white coat. It was Fiona. There was a snarl of anger behind Alex. He whirled around. Das had also seen Fiona. He whipped up his arm and fired off a shot as she scampered toward the chapel. The shot passed low over her head and exploded against one the standing stones. Das took deliberate aim for the next shot. Alex scooped up a chunk of icy snow and threw it toward the alien. It struck Das full in the face. He staggered back firing off a shot that streaked harmlessly into the sky. Jim, following Alex's example, threw another snowball that struck Das in the chest. Alex looked toward the chapel. Fiona was now only a few yards from the ruin. A blue energy ball streaked past Alex's head and exploded against a door pillar. Fiona let out a muffled scream of pain, staggered the last few feet and collapsed out of sight through the entrance.

Alex started to run toward the chapel. There was a deep rumbling in the core of Jake's Law. The ground shuddered beneath his feet. He stumbled and toppled to the ground. A blue energy ball streaked two feet over his head.

The spacecraft still hung ominously motionless, two hundred feet above, like a giant umbrella, sheltering the ground below it from the falling snow. Then Alex's ear picked up a low pulsing sound vibrating the air around him. He looked toward the chapel. A bright glow inside the ruin was already spilling out of the windows and casting dark jagged shadows of its broken walls across the snow-covered summit. The pulsing sound was increasing along with the brightness of the glow. There was a sudden flare up of light and then darkness. The pulsing sound had also gone, replaced by the gentle moan of the winter wind, driving swirling flurries of powder snow across the frozen summit.

Suddenly, a shimmering column of pale blue light streaked upward from the center of the chapel. Alex looked up. The beam of light speared the underbelly of the spacecraft. Waves of reddish orange light rippled across its silver surface as it tore free from the impaling beacon and started to accelerate erratically upward. There was brilliant flash of light, followed by a distant muffled explosion. A flurry of flaming objects cascaded toward earth, one by one to disappear. High up above, a circular cloud of gas spread like an incandescent halo in the dark sky.

Alex scrambled to his feet. The blue beacon of light still pointed up into the heavens. A rumbling sound brought his eyes back to earth. One end of the chapel had collapsed. A crack appeared in the ground at the base of the crumbled wall and was rapidly spreading like a giant, dark, ragged tear across the snow-covered summit, growing wider and deeper with every yard. Then Alex saw Das, still staring up into the heavens at the fading cloud of gas that marked the demise of the space craft, oblivious to the ever widening fissure carving its way across the summit's surface toward him. At the last minute Das became aware of the danger. He frantically scrambled to jump clear, lost his footing and with a blood chilling scream, he tumbled into the crevice.

There was a rumbling sound from deep within the core of the law. The ground around Alex began to shake and shudder. Alex staggered as the ground below his feet dropped a few inches then silence fell. The ground tremors had ceased. Alex turned to see Jim standing twenty yards away, still staring upward. A large object swept between them. It was the sphere.

Alex threw himself backwards. A whirlpool of snow was sucked up from the ground. Alex, buffeted by swirling air currents, cupped his hands to his eyes. The sphere spiraled up into the heavens and vanished into the darkness. Then, the blue light of the beacon suddenly disappeared. A giant inverted cone of clear air had been carved out of the falling snow by the rapid ascent of the sphere. It was like standing under the dome of some massive, open-air cathedral.

Snowflakes began drifting down to reclaim the space and lightly settled on Alex's upturned face. Then he remembered Jim. He looked to where he had last seen him. There was no sign of him. Only a carpet of snow bearing the indentation of the sphere's take off. Then there was a disturbance on the surface of the snow. A ghostly hand broke through, followed by another. A head and shoulders followed.

"Jim!" Alex started to run toward the struggling figure. Jim raised himself up, dusting the snow from his clothes.

"I just about got flattened. It missed me by inches." He took a deep breath. "I saw my face in it as it went by." He looked around. "Where's Fiona?" Alex scrambled to his feet and ran toward the ruined chapel. He slowed up short of the doorway, frightened at what he would find. She lay like a rag doll on the chapel floor. Blood stains tinged the fresh snowflakes melting on her upturned face. A faint and rapidly fading greenish glow still illuminated the trigstone hole in the chapel floor. Alex gently lifted up Fiona's hands. The scorched remains of her leather gloves adhered to the blistered skin.

"Is she dead?" Jim stood framed in the chapel door, his face almost as white as the powdered snow that covered his clothes.

Alex looked up at Jim. "I can see her breath. She's alive." Fiona's eyes flickered and she gave a mild groan.

"She's coming round," said Jim.

Fiona's eyes were now wide open. She raised her right hand and gingerly touched her bleeding temple. "Sus? What happened to Sus?"

Alex put his hands on her shoulders. "Sus is okay, Fiona. He is heading home."

She sat up straight. "Das? What about Das?"

"He's gone for good, Fiona. We're safe."

Fiona looked puzzled. "How did it all happen?"

Alex helped her back onto her feet. "You did it Fiona. We'll explain it later. It's a wee bit complicated."

Jim patted her on the back. "You did not bad… for a girl." He grinned. "You took out the UFO as well as Das. You got two birds with one trigstone."

The sound of police sirens wailed from the valley below.

Alex took hold of Fiona's arm. "Let's get out of here."

CHAPTER 27

"**W**ATTS! WATTS! ARE YOU DREAMING boy?**"** Alex jumped in his seat and a snigger of laughter rippled through the classroom. Mr. Rae, the lean and mean math teacher, who, over the years, had spared no effort to earn his nickname, Killer Rae, stomped from behind his desk and down the aisle. He rested both hands on Alex's desk and leaned forward until his long, angular nose was but a few inches from Alex's face. "Good of you to rejoin us back here on planet Earth, Watts." A fresh outbreak of titters rippled through the class only to be instantly frozen by a sweeping glare from the teacher.

"Sorry, sir... I was thinking about something."

"You seem to have done a lot of thinking since you came back from holiday. Too much rich food was it. Too much Christmas pudding?"

This time a few restrained laughs were rewarded by a faint smirk from Killer Rae. Alex looked across the room. Jim gave him a sympathetic look. "I've had something personal on my mind, sir... I'm sorry... It won't happen again."

The teacher stood erect. "Make sure it doesn't." He turned and strode back to his desk. As the lesson dragged on, Alex strained to keep up his concentration. It was not easy. His thoughts drifted again back to that last night on Jake's Law several weeks ago

When Mr. Dickson arrived at the village police station on that eventful night, he had found it deserted. Every officer on duty and those off duty had been called out to cope with the sporadic outbreaks of strike protests and violence that had erupted throughout the night. The explosion that had occurred when the ambulance had collided with Das's car had been seen by several people, including Mr. Dickson. He drove fast toward Jacob's Law and came upon Fiona, Alex, and Jim scrambling down the hillside, all exhausted and cold. He whisked them away from the scene just minutes before the police and emergency units arrived. Safely back at the manse, they all agreed that they should, for the moment, keep their involvement in the night's events to themselves.

The police inquiries identified the ambulance as having been stolen from the hospital. A miner's union representative, on a late night walk home from the protest at the pit, swore he had seen Mr. Steel driving a car toward Jake's Law. The car was found smashed to pieces at the foot of the law. Two bodies were found inside the car that had been recognized as members of one of the flying picket groups, but no positive identification had been made. As for Mr. Steel, an intensive local search did not locate the union official. Bloodstains in the car suggested the possibility that he had been injured and may have suffered concussion and memory loss. The authorities initiated a nationwide missing person search, but without success.

The official geologist report on the ground subsidence

and slope failure on Jake's Law suggested that the fracturing of the rock was likely due to mineral settlement of old mine workings below the law as well as the structural weakness brought on by all the quarry blasting that had taken place in the past.

The Edinburgh negotiations between the union and the coal board reached a settlement. The day after Christmas, the strike was over. Some media commentators said that Mr. Steel's absence, however tragic the circumstances, had been a prime factor in the resolution of the dispute.

Life in the village began to return to some semblance of normal. The Dicksons met with Alex, Jim, and Fiona to discuss preparations for the confrontation with Tan's fleet. The stable's attic was chosen as the most suitable and secure place to set up their "battle station," as Mr. Dickson dubbed it. They obtained second hand video game consoles, "Invasion Earth" cartridges and TV sets to bring them up to the required number. The TV sets, all shapes and sizes, managed to fit quite well on a broad storage shelf along one wall of the loft. Some old school desks, stored in the loft for many years, were pulled out, dusted off, and placed before the TV sets. The video consoles and controls were placed on these.

There was only one electrical plug point in the loft, but Mr. Dickson obtained an adapter, which allowed all units to be hooked up. It was the first day of the New Year before they were ready to try out the battle station.

All five, Alex, Jim, Fiona, and her parents, took their places at the desks. They all plugged in the game cassettes. One by one the titles flickered onto the screens. They had turned down the sound volume. The silence added to the eeriness in the dusty gloom of the loft, as "Invasion Earth" appeared on each screen. Alex sat in a central position. He was the first to place his "pearl" on the console. A restrained cheer had burst out as the screen displayed the star pierced blackness of space. The others followed suit. They began to try out the controls, just as Sus had shown them. Their initial hesitancy gradually eased, as they grew more adept in the use of the controls. They practiced as much as they could each day.

Sus had indicated that the interception date could be early January. Each of them carried one of the pearls with them at all times. As the weeks passed, they began to stay closer to the church and to the battle station. They set up a shift system so that one person was always in the loft with Fiona's parents, sharing the night shift periods, but nothing happened. The pearls did not glow. The screen continued to show empty space.

The sixth of January passed, then the seventh, and then the eighth. Still no sign of Tan's fleet. School had started, so it was left to the Dicksons to monitor the battle station during the main part of the day. Some church members directed pointed questions at Mr. Dickson regarding the time he spent in the loft. He explained that he was carrying out a special surprise children's project.

The grey days of January slipped by. Still, there was no sign of Tan's invasion fleet.

Killer Rae's voice droned on as his squeaking chalk traced out a geometric solution on the dusty blackboard. Across the already grey sky, a distant rumble of thunder gave notice of an approaching storm. Alex turned his attention back to copying the teacher's scribbles into his notebook. He heard the sound of running feet in the corridor. The classroom door burst open. Fiona stood there, gasping for breath.

Killer Rae threw down his chalk and glared at the intruder. "What on earth do you think you are doing, girl?" Fiona ignored him as her eyes fixed on Alex. He needed no words to understand. He stuck his hand into his pocket and pulled out a matchbox. His fingers trembled as he pulled out the tray. The pearl, cushioned in cotton wool, was glowing. Alex jumped to his feet. Jim was already moving. Alex ran toward the door, knocking books and pencils off desks as he went. Killer Rae stood, wideeyed, rooted to the spot as Alex ran past him and almost collided with Jim at the door as they exited the room. As he ran down the corridor after Jim and Fiona, Alex glanced over his shoulder. Killer Rae had stepped out of the classroom and had grabbed the intercom phone just outside the door. They ran out the school entrance and across the playground to the bicycle shed. They cycled through the main gate as Simpson, the school janitor, clattered down the entrance steps. As they sped through the village streets, the sky above grew darker. A flash of lightning split the gloom, followed by the clash of thunder. Large raindrops splattered down. Their bike wheels hissed along the wet pavement. Startled pedestrians jumped back as the cyclists streaked past. The rainfall turned into a deluge when they reached the church. The gravel crunched beneath their tires as they dashed toward the stables. They threw their bikes against the wall and scrambled up the stairs. Lightning cut through the sky above them. The instant clap of thunder vibrated the wooden steps under their feet. Fiona reached the top and beat on the door. There was a scraping sound from inside the loft. "Who is it?"

"It's us, Dad. Let us in. We are soaked."

A key turned. The door opened a crack. Mr. Dickson's face appeared. He looked very tense. "Thank goodness! We were getting rather worried." He pulled the door wide and they bustled in out of the rain. Mrs. Dickson was seated in front of one of the two illuminated TV screens. Both had glowing pearls on top of the consoles. She gave a nervous smile.

Alex glanced up at the screens. They both showed the same picture of black space. He turned to Mr. Dickson. "Where is Tan's fleet?"

The minister rubbed his chin with the back of his hand. "They don't show up at the moment...but they must be out there."

Alex sat down at the central console and pushed the cassette into place. The game titles flickered onto the colored screen. "INVASION EARTH." The electronic voice sounded out the familiar theme. "WELCOME DEFENDER...EARTH IS BEING INVADED..."

CHAPTER 28

THE GAME VOICE STOPPED. ALEX took the matchbox from his pocket and lifted out the small, glowing pearl sphere. He placed it carefully atop the console. The graphics of the video game were replaced by the velvet, star pierced blackness of space. There was no sign of Tan's invading fleet.

"Some of the stars seem to be bigger," said Fiona. "Look at the size of that one straight ahead."

Mr. Dickson stood up and came over to Alex's screen which was the biggest and had the sharpest picture. "I think that is our sun, Fiona, and it has been getting bigger by the minute. We are approaching our solar system fast. We must catch up with Tan's ships before the Asteroid Belt."

"What asteroid belt?" said Jim.

Mr. Dickson tapped the screen. "It's a band of planetary debris that encircles the sun, between Mars and Jupiter."

"It's a lot of rocks?" said Jim.

Mr. Dickson nodded. "Millions of rocks, Jim. Some are hundreds of miles in diameter, but they vary in size all the way down to pebbles and grains of sand."

"Will Tan's fleet be able to get through, Dad?" said Fiona.

"It's not quite as dense as that, Fiona. A space ship could

be navigated through without hitting any really large piece, but if we have to dogfight in that zone, it would be tricky. Like playing football in a forest."

"Tan will have the same problem," said Alex.

Mr. Dickson nodded. "That's true; but we can only see what is straight ahead and the commanders of his ships will be able to see 360." He gave a grim smile. "On the plus side, we do have the advantage of surprise. They will not be expecting an attack. After that, it will be a bit of a shambles."

Silence fell in the loft. They exchanged nervous glances. Rain hammered down on the tiles above them. Alex looked up. A drop of water landed on his forehead. He dried it off with his coat sleeve. A flash of white light pierced the cracks in the door and a cannon-like thunderclap shook the whole building. The single light bulb dimmed and flickered.

"That was a close one!" said Mr. Dickson.

"Stuart! Stuart!" Rose Dickson was staring at her TV screen. Alex whirled around to look at his screen. Mr. Dickson was beside him. "It looks like our wait is over." Alex swallowed hard. There was no mistaking the cluster of bright objects in the center of the screen. As he watched, the points of light began to take on more definite shape. Another clash of thunder rattled the tiles above. Mr. Dickson slapped his hands together. "Action stations everybody!" He turned to Alex. " I want you to lead the attack, Alex." Alex was about to protest when Fiona spoke up. "Dad's right, Alex." Jim nodded in agreement.

Fiona turned to her father. "We need a prayer, Dad."

"We do indeed." He lifted his hands, palms up. "Lord, we have what would seem an impossible task ahead of us. David also looked small and pathetic as he faced Goliath. We pray that your strength would inhabit our weakness as we take on the evil forces of Tan. We ask this the name of our Lord and Savior, Jesus Christ. Amen." A roll of thunder punctuated the prayer.

Alex slipped into his seat. The formation of Tan's fleet of ships was now quite clear, two curved "v" shapes, six ships in each, like a flock of wild geese heading south for the winter, but these were no wild geese. The individual ships were diamond shaped and dull red. The two v's lay close to each other, forming a rough "M." Between them was a larger craft, also diamondshaped, but elongated like a kite. It was obviously Tan's flagship. It was a deeper, more luminous red, than the others. The formation of thirteen ships looked like some grotesque playing card against the blackness of space. Alex looked to his left. Mr. Dickson was nearest, then his wife. On Alex's right were Jim and Fiona.

Mr. Dickson turned to him. "How should we tackle this, Alex?"

"I think our best chance is to split them up between us, just as we are sitting. Mrs. Dickson, takes the first three on the left, you the next three. Jim can take the first three on the right and Fiona the next three." He ran the tip of his tongue over his dry lips. "The big one in the middle must be Tan's ship... I will take it."

Mr. Dickson nodded his head. "That should do it." He cleared his throat. "Once we open fire, it will become a free for all. Everybody will just have to take their chances and remember..." He smiled as he looked at everyone, "...if the ship isn't diamondshaped, don't fire." A few nervous giggles were drowned by another tile shaking thunderclap.

Alex's stomach was churning, as the enemy ships on his screen grew larger by the second. He shivered and suddenly became aware of his rain soaked clothes. He pulled out his handkerchief and wiped the sweat from his hands. He took hold of the control joystick in his right hand and rested his right thumb lightly on the red "fire" button.

Alex raised his left hand above his head. "Okay, everyone take aim. When I count to three, fire." He joggled the stick to put Tan's flagship in the center of his screen and began to count. "One...Two...Three..." A crash of thunder blotted out his last words.

Alex jumped in his seat as he pressed the red button. Balls of blue light streaked away on the screen toward the invasion fleet. The farthest right of Tan's ships vanished in a pulsating cloud of scarlet fire.

Jim let out a shout of triumph. Another explosion enveloped the screen. The diamond-shaped ships broke formation like wild birds when a hunting shotgun goes off and scattered in every direction. Tan's flagship had peeled away to the right and Alex's first shot streaked harmlessly into space. He locked on to another ship and punched the button. The blue ball of energy streaked right into the center of the red diamond. A brilliant flash of flame caused Alex to blink. He tried to lock on another one, which started to pull away. He waggled the stick to follow it. The screen was suddenly full of ships. Balls of blue light crisscrossed the screen. A wedge shaped craft streaked past with two diamond ships in pursuit. Blue fireballs streaked toward the wedge ship. It disappeared in a pulsating cloud of flame.

"My screen has gone... I've no picture," Mr. Dickson shouted out. The minister's screen was just snow. The pearl on top of the console no longer glowed. Another clap of thunder shook the loose roof tiles. Alex was jostling to lock onto one of the diamond ships. He saw no sign of Tan's flagship. Mrs. Dickson gave a squeal of elation. Another ball of scarlet flame pulsated on the screen. Alex at last got his quarry on center. He punched the button. The red diamond disintegrated. A ball of light streaked past him from behind. He pulled the joystick back. Another diamond appeared in front of him as it overshot. He stabbed at the button. The alien ship exploded in flames. He pulled his ship around in a wide sweeping turn. Fewer spacecraft showed up on the screen. No sign of Tan's flagship. Alex swung his ship in another direction.

Mr. Dickson was at his shoulder. "They got Rose. You three are on your own." Alex gritted his teeth and fired off another energy ball. A diamond ship jinked away to one side. The shot missed. Alex punched the button and the second shot struck the tail of an enemy ship. It spun off into space, breaking up as it went. He began another sweep. The screen showed no sign of movement. No enemy ships. He glanced to the right. Jim's screen was still operating. Beyond, he could see the disconsolate face of Fiona. Only two left now, but where were the enemy ships?

"Have we got them all?" Mr. Dickson looked around at the others. "How many did we destroy?"

"One for me," said Mrs. Dickson.

"Three," said Jim.

"One for me," said Fiona.

Mr. Dickson turned to Alex. "I got two, how about you."

"Four."

Mr. Dickson counted on his fingers. "Eleven...that means there are two left."

Alex looked around. "Did anyone get the flagship?" Everyone stayed silent. He turned back to the screen. "Tan is still out there."

The others crowded around behind Alex and Jim as they joggled their controls searching the black screens for the remaining enemy ships. Silence fell inside the loft. Over their heads, the rain pattered on the roof tiles.

"Look! There!" Fiona shouted out, pointing at Alex's screen. All eyes followed her outstretched finger. Two objects had appeared in the top righthand corner of the screen. Alex moved the control stick and brought the objects dead center.

"I've got them!" shouted Jim. "It's them alright. One is bigger than the other, don't you see?" A flash of lightning lit up the cracks in the door followed by another thunderclap which shook the loft. The picture on Alex's screen flickered. Then it shrunk into a narrow band before popping back to full size. Alex took a deep breath.

"Let's get them, Jim." The two enemy ships were getting closer. Tan's flagship was in front of the smaller ship. Suddenly, the rear ship swooped off in a wide turn. It headed straight for them.

"Look out! He's coming at you," Mr. Dickson warned.

Alex punched his "fire" button just as blue lights streaked toward him from the diamond ship. He broke away in a curving turn to the left. Then he saw Jim's wedge shaped craft and the diamond ship heading straight for each other. Blue flames streaked between the two. Jim yelled and Alex's screen was flooded with a pulsating cloud of fire. Alex turned to Jim's screen. It was blank. The pearl on the console did not glow.

"We've collided!" Jim groaned.

The fire cloud disappeared from Alex's screen. Dead ahead was the luminous red of Tan's giant flagship. Mr. Dickson put his hand on his shoulder. "One more to go, Alex. It's all up to you."

Alex nodded, but did not speak. He wiggled the joystick till the flagship was dead center. He waited for the enemy ship to turn. It did not. Then he saw something take shape on the starsprinkled blackness of space. A planet. At first he thought it was Earth, but as he got closer, he could see it was yellow with parallel belts of reddish brown.

"What is it?" said Jim

"If I'm not mistaken, that is Jupiter," said Mr. Dickson quietly. He turned to Alex. "Beyond Jupiter is the asteroid belt. You must destroy Tan before he gets there, Alex."

Alex chewed his lower lip as he concentrated on the fleeing flagship. The giant red ship drifted toward the center of the screen. His finger hovered over the "fire" button. A tremendous clap of thunder boomed overhead. The TV screen went blank. Alex whirled round. The loft was in darkness.

"Oh, no!" Mr. Dickson groaned. "It's a power cut! The storm has cut the power." Alex slumped in his seat. A wave of nausea swept over him. There was nothing left to stop Tan. Earth was doomed.

CHAPTER 29

M<small>R. DICKSON PULLED OPEN THE</small> loft door and stepped out onto the landing. Another roll of thunder rumbled through the overcast skies. The rain drizzled down as Alex and the others joined him.

"What do we do now?" said Fiona.

Her father shrugged his shoulders. "Wait for the power to come back, I suppose."

A flash of lightning lit up the clouds on the horizon beyond the village. Fiona started counting. "One, two, three, four..." She stopped as the distant thunder rumbled. "That was four miles." She was about to say something else then stopped. She grabbed her father's arm. "The village street lights are on." She turned to Alex. "That means the power is still on there."

Alex stared at her for a second, and then ran back into the darkened loft. He found the way to his desk, guided by the faint glow of the pearl. He picked it up and quickly put it into the matchbox. He ran back out the door. The others jumped out of his way as he descended the steps two at a time. "Where are you going?" shouted Jim as he clattered down the steps after Alex.

"The Video Games Café," shouted Alex as he hauled his bike upright. Within seconds, he was pedaling furiously out of the church gates and down the road toward the village. He glanced over his shoulder. Jim was coming after him, standing up on the pedals. Alex kept his head down to reduce drag. He reached the village and turned down a side street. A small car coming toward him suddenly braked and swung across, blocking most of the road. Alex managed to sneak past, but not before he recognized the driver of the car as Simpson, the school janitor.

Alex glanced back. Jim was still behind him. The car was doing a three-point turn. Alex pedaled harder than ever. In his mind he could see the giant red flagship getting closer and closer to Earth and, behind it, his lone fighter ship, travelling blindly through space. He took another sharp turn down a side street and his rear wheel drifted out. He wobbled for several yards before he regained his balance. The storm seemed to have passed over. He took a short cut along a pathway between two buildings. Three women, walking together with full shopping bags, jumped screaming to the side as he zigzagged between them. An object flew past his ear and bounced along the ground in front of him. It was a large onion. The shouts of anger faded behind him as he passed between two more buildings and bounced over the curb onto another street. The neon sign, "Video Games Café," flickered through the grey gloom. He braked to a halt and jumped off all in the same movement. He lifted his bike over the curb and leaned it against the building. There was the whirr of bicycle wheels. Jim drew up beside him. His ear was splattered with red. "Did you fall off and bust your ear?" said Alex, as he ran toward the entrance.

Jim dabbed at his ear with his handkerchief. "One of those

old birds threw a tomato at me. That's what we get for trying to save the world."

Alex was already pushing open the café door. The smell of burnt coffee and overheated meat pies hit his nostrils. A group of youths sat at one of the tables and a couple of younger children were playing the video games. Mrs. Black, complete with a drooping cigarette hanging from her lips and nicotine tinted kiss curl, glowered at the newcomers through a cloud of espresso steam. "Shut the door behind you! It costs money to heat this place you know." Jim closed the door. Alex ran to the video games. Two younger children were playing the video games but the "Invasion Earth" was free. Still breathing heavily, he pulled out the matchbox. The pearl was still glowing. His ship had not been destroyed.

He stuck his hand in his pocket and took out the coins. He turned to Jim. "Do you have ten pence?"

Jim raised his eyebrows, stuck his hand in one pocket, then the other. He shook his head. "I'm skint. The wifie will give you change."

Alex looked at the coins. "I've only got eight pence." He went to the counter. The cigarette end glowed through the steam.

"What is it kid?" The pudgy face appeared, as the steam drifted away, like clouds from Mount Rushmore.

"Could you oblige me with a ten pence piece?"

The register bell sounded out as the cash drawer opened and her sausage like fingers pulled out the coin. "You must be the last of the big spenders. Are you sure one will be enough?" She exchanged a smirk with the youths at the table.

Alex laid out his money on the greasy counter top. "Well, the fact is I only have eight pence, but I will bring the other two pence later."

The sausage fingers threw the coin back into the tray and slammed the drawer shut. "Do you think this is the Salvation Army?"

Jim stepped forward. "Och, come on, missus. You can trust us to bring the rest later. Its only two pence and it is for a very good cause."

"I'm not in this business for kindness, laddie, and I'm not Mother Teresa either, so buzz off and scrounge your video money from somebody else." She vanished into a cloud of steam, heading for the storeroom.

Jim shook his head. "I can't believe it. We're going to lose the world cause we're short tuppence."

Alex turned to look at the youths. One of them flicked back a lock of greasy hair, then picked a ten pence coin up from the table and held it out toward Alex.

Alex reached out his hand, "Gee thanks, I..."

The youth pulled back his hand and he and his friends burst into raucous laughter. He stood up and once more held out his hand, but with a clenched fist. "How much is it worth to you, kid?" He turned to smirk at his friends then back to Alex. "Come on kid...make me an offer."

Alex cast a desperate look at the "Invasion Earth" game. It was still vacant. He turned back. "I have a ten speed Raleigh outside." That provoked another bout of laughter. "Come outside and see for yourself."

The youth slowly stood up and headed for the door. Chairs scraped along the floor as his friends followed. Outside they gathered around Alex's bike.

The youth stared at it then back at Alex. "You're having me on kid. How would you like a punch up the nose?"

Alex stuck out his hand. "Give me the ten pence and the bike's yours."

The youth blinked several times. He looked at the bike then back to Alex. He pushed the greasy copper coin into Alex's hand and jumped onto the bike and peddled off with his friends running in full cry behind him. Alex heard the sound of a high revving car engine. A small car raced down the road toward them.

"It's Simpson!" Jim took hold of Alex's arm. "Get in there. I will try to draw him away."

Alex whirled around and ran for the café door. As he pulled it open and jumped in, he saw Jim peddling furiously down the center of the street with the car in hot pursuit. Alex ran to the video game, brushing past the waitress who was wiping down a table. She swiped at him with the wet cloth. "You're a real addict, kid. You should get the doctor to check you out."

Alex bumped against tables and chairs as he scrambled to the "Invasion Earth" video game. He took the still glowing pearl from the matchbox and placed it on the control panel. It stayed put, as if magnetized. He pushed in the coin and pressed the start button. The screen went yellow. There was no velvet blackness of space. No red flagship. Just a dirty yellow.

Of course! Jupiter. It was Jupiter. His fighter ship was diving straight into the planet Jupiter. He pulled the joystick back hard. Nothing seemed to happen. He saw brown bands in the yellow. He pulled the stick full to the left. A dark area began to form in the top right corner of the screen. It continued to grow, getting darker all the time. The boundary between the dark and the yellow was curved. He pulled the stick back to center. The yellow outline of Jupiter dropped down. It was replaced with the star-pierced darkness of space.

He breathed a sigh of relief. Where was Tan's flagship?

Which direction was Earth? Then he saw a small glowing circle, the sun. It had to be the sun. It was smaller than he had ever seen it, but then he was further away. If he aimed for the sun he would be heading for Earth. He jockeyed with the joystick until the bright orb was dead center. Something glinted in the distance. He moved the stick to follow it. There was another twinkle of reflected light. It was the flagship. The giant red kite shaped craft grew larger by the second. Sweat formed on his brow, as the flagship moved closer and closer. The café doorbell jingled. The flagship was now dead center. His finger hovered over the 'fire' button.

Suddenly rough hands grabbed his shoulders and hauled him away from the controls. "Got you, you little scruff." Alex yelled as he turned to see his assailant, Simpson, the school janitor. Stained teeth formed a grin of triumph. Alex struggled to get free, but to no avail. Simpson started to hustle him toward the door.

A small, red haired boy, tried to enter. "Get out of the way, lad." The janitor growled out. It was Bert, who had helped Alex and Sus escape from McCracken and his men. Bert stepped aside and gave Alex a sympathetic glance. The janitor pushed Alex outside. "I don't know what got into to you, Watts, but I'm sure the headmaster will be interested."

Alex grabbed hold of the janitor's arm. "You must let me go back, Mr. Simpson, you must...."

"Are you crazy, Watts? Get in the car." Alex was bundled through the open passenger door of the two-door car into the back seat. The door slammed shut.

Jim was already sitting there, blood seeping through the torn knee of his trousers. "Did you get him, Alex? Did you get Tan?"

Alex clenched his teeth to keep back tears of frustration.

He couldn't speak the words. Jim's crestfallen face signified he understood. The janitor went round to the driver's seat. Alex closed his eyes and let his head flop against the back of the seat. There was a light tap on the window. He opened his eyes. It was Bert. He gestured with his hand for Alex to open the window. The janitor was busy putting his key in the ignition

Alex carefully wound down the window. "What is it, Bert?"

Bert's face radiated admiration. "Did you guys skip school to play video games?"

Alex sighed. "You could say that, Bert."

The boy's face beamed brighter. "Magic! " He held out his hand. "Is this yours? I found it on the game." In his open hand was the pearl. It was not glowing.

Alex slid his hand out the narrow opening. "Yes, it's mine...thanks."

The boy carefully handed it over. "How does it do that?"

"Do what?" said Alex.

"Glow like it did. How does it do that?"

Alex looked at the boy. "When did it stop glowing?"

"Just when I finished the new game."

"What new game?" asked Alex?

"The new 'Invasion Earth.' The one you were playing."

Alex sat up straight. "How did the game finish?"

The boy gave him a quizzical look. "When I knocked off the big red ship, of course."

Alex swallowed hard. "You destroyed the red ship?"

Bert grinned. "Of course, I did. Piece of cake. It was a smashing explosion. I got a wee bit too close though. My ship got taken out in the blow back from the explosion. Terrific graphics. Best I've ever seen. But the screen went black. It's dumb. Going to all that trouble making up a great new game like that, and not giving your score." Alex and Jim slammed back in their seats as the janitor let out the clutch and the car accelerated off down the street.

Alex grabbed Jim's arm. "We did it, Jim. We destroyed Tan's fleet."

Jim gasped, "How?"

"Wee Bert took out Tan's flagship."

"You're kidding?"

"When Simpson dragged me out of the café, Bert found the game was still playing." Alex grinned. "He just picked up where I left off."

"He didn't know it was for real?"

"No! He thought it was a new version of the game with better graphics."

Jim shook his head. "He saved the world and he doesn't know it." Jim banged his fist on the seat cushion. "We're all going to be famous, Alex."

Alex shook his head. "I don't think so, Jim."

Jim's jaw dropped. "What are you talking about?"

"Nobody knows we did it, Jim. Nobody knows who Sus was. Nobody knows about an alien invasion."

Jim was stunned into silence for a moment or two. He sighed. "You're right."

We have no proof. They will think we are all crazy."

Alex forced a grin. "Don't forget Sus though, Jim. If he made it home, we'll be heroes on Planet Ven."

Jim sighed. "It's not the same as watching it on BBC and reading it in the newspapers, is it?"

"Sus said that one day there will be contact between his civilization and Earth. Then people here will know."

Jim rolled his eyes. "Give me a break, Alex. It will be years and years before that happens. We might be collecting the old age pension by that time."

The car turned off the road, passed though the school gate, and pulled up at the main door. Simpson switched off the engine and turned around to look at them. "Stay in the car and don't move. I'm going to get Mr. Rae." He's looking forward to escorting you up to the headmaster's office." He stepped out the car, slamming the door shut behind him and vanished into the building.

There was a period of quiet as they sat slumped down in the back seat. Alex was pondering the sudden switch from the elation of victory and the anticlimax of their present situation.

Jim broke the silence. "Did you see that 'Battle of Britain' movie on telly last week?"

Alex nodded. "What about it?"

"At the end of the movie, they had Churchill's speech. The 'Never was so much owed by so many to so few' bit?"

"So what?"

Jim shrugged. "I just thought we were a few who helped save the world and Mrs. Thatcher won't be making any speeches about us in the House of Commons."

Alex sighed. "That's for sure...." The sentence was cut off as a flickering light caught his eye. He opened his hand. The pearl lay there on his open palm, glowing; not with the steady glow of before, but with a pulsing, intermittent flashing on and off.

"What's happening?" gasped Jim.

"I don't know," whispered Alex.

"It looks like Morse code," said Jim. "We should write it down." He stuck his hand into the door pocket. "There's a pen, but no paper."

"I'll read it out, Jim. Write it on your hand."

"Okay! Okay!"

"Dot-dot-dot-dash...Dot-dot-dot-dash ...Dot-dot-dot-dash Dash dot dash-dot... Dot-dot- dash...Dot-dash-dot-dot Dot-dot-dot...Dot-dot-dash...Dot-dot-dot."

The pearl stopped glowing. Jim extended his open palm to Alex, "Can you read it? You were in the Scouts."

Alex placed the pearl back in the matchbox and stuffed it in his pocket, "I'll have a go. Give me the pen." He started to read the markings on Jim's palm and write on the palm of his own hand. He stopped and stared at what he had written. "Gee Whiz!"

"What is it?" Jim's voice croaked with impatient excitement.

Alex looked up. "You're not going to believe this."

International Morse Code

1. A dash is equal to three dots.
2. The space between parts of the same letter is equal to one dot.
3. The space between two letters is equal to three dots.
4. The space between two words is equal to seven dots.

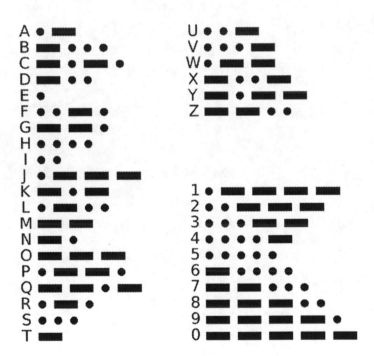